CANDID TALES

INDIA ON A MOTORCYCLE

CANDID TALES

INDIA ON A MOTORCYCLE

ADITHI RAO

ILLUSTRATIONS BY RUCHI SHAH

HarperCollins*Children'sBooks*

First published in India in 2020 by HarperCollins Children's Books
An imprint of HarperCollins *Publishers*

HarperCollins Publishers India, Cyber City, Building 10-A, Gurugram,
Haryana-122002, India
www.harpercollins.co.in

2 4 6 8 10 9 7 5 3 1

P-ISBN: 978-93-5357-640-0

Typeset in Cormorant 12pt/ 15.8 by
Manipal Technology Limited, Manipal

Printed and bound at
MicroPrints India, New Delhi

MIX
Paper
FSC
FSC® C218906

This product is made of FSC®-certified and other controlled material.

HarperCollins Publishers, Macken House, 39/40 Mayor Street
Upper, Dublin 1, D01 C9W8, Ireland

For Latha, Haripriya and Anamika,
"foul-weather" friends, always so dear

&

Dr. Mohan Rao,
who makes all things complete.

INTRODUCTION

Candida Louis was born in 1990, to an Anglo-Indian family in Hubballi, Karnataka. After completing her education from Sacred Heart Convent School and then Oxford College, Hubballi, she joined the finance department of a leading multi-national company. After five years (that felt like ten!) in the IT industry, she finally discovered what she did *not* want to do: Sit behind a desk inside the four walls of an office from 9 a.m. to 9 p.m. every day!

What she did want to do was travel.

She handed in her resignation, and embarked upon a solo journey across India on a motorcycle. Twice. The first time was in 2015, when she was on the road for three months. The second time, in 2016, was for four. In all, she covered some 32,000 kilometres through 22 states and ... well, she lost count of how many cities!

She now works as a travel consultant, and conducts motorcycle tours for travel enthusiasts across the world. She also runs her own travel company (www.candidalouis.com). Candida currently lives in Bangalore with her terrace garden and two cats. She describes herself as: Blogger. Influencer. Adventurer.

She can be found @candidalouis on Instagram, Facebook and YouTube.

LEARNING TO FLY

LEARNING TO FLY

Childhood in Hubballi

'Daniel, Candi won't stop crying,' murmured Joanna, shaking her husband awake while rocking the baby in the crook of her arm. Daniel stirred. He opened his eyes and blinked up into the light. His wife's worried face came into focus at the same moment that his little daughter's cries hit his ears full blast. Sitting bolt upright in bed, Daniel held out his arms. Joanna passed the little bundle of blankets and baby into them, and sank down on the bed beside him with a tired sigh.

Daniel felt Baby Candida's forehead. Warm, but only little-baby-warm. No fever then. Nappy? Dry. Tummy? Full. He ran his finger along her gum and felt a slight roughness there before Candi clamped her mouth gleefully over the friendly finger and began to chew vigorously. Aaha! So *that* was the problem!

'New tooth coming, Jo. That's what's bothering Baby.'

'But what do we do, Dan? We can't let her cry the whole night!'

Daniel looked at his wife thoughtfully. He looked down at Candi. The novelty of chomping on his finger had worn off and she was readying herself for another round of bawling. The little face screwed up, the eyes filled with tears, she took a nice deep breath and opened her mouth wide ...

'Don't even think about it, young lady!' cried her father, wagging a finger at her. Candi blinked in surprise, momentarily distracted from her purpose. Daniel catapulted off the bed, caught up the key to his motorbike and ran out the front door of the tiny house, taking wife and 8-month-old daughter with him.

He kick-started the bike while Joanna stood by, watching with bemused eyes. Candi, no longer impressed by the flurry of activity, had gone back to screaming in her mother's arms.

'Well, what are you waiting for, darling?' urged Daniel.

What indeed, thought Joanna, who was, by now, desperate enough to try anything. She climbed on behind her husband. Daniel carefully manoeuvred the bike out through the narrow, iron gate. Every house in the colony of Nehru Nagar in the city of Hubballi seemed fast asleep. Not a light shone in any of the windows. The only illumination came from the street lights that intermittently and haphazardly lined the streets.

At the end of the lane, Daniel accelerated, and vroooo...m, the bike sped away! Candi abruptly stopped crying. She blinked up at her mother. Joanna shifted her from the crook of her arm to an upright position, wedging the infant firmly between her own body and Daniel's. The wind hit little Candi full in the face, and she gave a gurgle of surprise.

'Daniel!' Joanna exclaimed joyfully, 'Dan, it's working! Baby's not crying anymore. She's *laughing*!'

Candida Louis cut twenty-six more teeth in the coming years. Never again did she spend another night crying.

When Candida was in second grade, the family shifted to Hilton Apartment in Vivekananda Colony. St Joseph's Church, where some families among Hubballi's small Anglo-Indian community worshipped, was as close to the new home as it had been to the old. The present one was bigger, and living in an apartment meant that Candi could play with the other children who also lived there. You would think that was the reason she was so happy, right? Wrong.

Candi was happy because she now lived walking distance from her best friend, Spike. Where they used to play together once a week after Sunday mass, they now met every evening and played with the children of Hilton Apartment. Soon they became part of a large gang of friends.

Candi was happy for another reason too. Her parents never stopped the bike rides. Ever since that fateful night, it had become a ritual, climbing onto the back of Daddy's Bullet, sandwiched cozily between her parents, feeling as if she was a bird in flight as they whizzed through the sleeping streets of Hubballi. They had nowhere to go, nothing to do and no reason to do it. They rode for the pure joy of it, because they loved the feel of the bike beneath them, the sky above them, and the wind in their faces!

Then, on Candi's seventh birthday, things got even better. After Spike and the gang had gobbled up the last of the chips and cake, and gone home, Daniel looked down at his daughter and said in mock seriousness, 'You're too old to sit about doing nothing. I want you up in the front of the bike with me, young lady. There's work for you to do.' The twinkle in his eye belied the frown on his brow. Candi grinned up at him eagerly.

'Climb onto the petrol tank!' he instructed. Her parents got on behind her, first Daddy, then Mamma. Daddy placed Candi's little hands on the bike handles (she had to lean way forward to reach them), and then kick-started the bike. Vroom, vroom, vroooooooooooom! The bike leapt forward, dancing to the left, then wobbling drunkenly to the right, as Candi went about her new task with more vigour and enthusiasm than skill. Joanna grabbed onto her husband's shoulders in alarm to keep from being thrown right off. But Daniel only laughed. A moment later, his hands covered Candi's, and in a trice the trusty old machine was back on course, where it remained for the rest of the ride.

And this was the ritual they followed every time. Every time until one day as they were riding cheerfully along ... Candida looked down and found that her father's hands were no longer holding the handles. Hers were the only ones there!

Eleven-year-old Candida ran down the steps of the temple tank of the Siddharudha Swamy Temple, armed with a clean glass jar.

'Be careful, darling!' called Joanna. Candida paid no attention because Mamma always called out those very same words, every time they rode here. Which was every Sunday. It was always the same: Mamma's words of caution. Candida now sat down on the bottom-most step, leaned forward and peered into the greenish water. Her sparkling eyes searched its murky depths eagerly for that one fish—the gold-and-orange one—that always caught her attention each time she fed the fishes in the tank of the Siddharudha Ashram. This fish was beautiful, and stood out among its grey companions who swam the length and breadth of that tank alongside it so diligently, day after day, year after year.

In a minute, there was a flash of gold and Candida knew that the moment had arrived. She dipped her jar into the water, in the path of the gold-and-orange fish, and it swam straight inside! In a flash, Candida lifted the jar out of the water. 'Timothy,' she mumbled to herself, giving the little fellow a name. Tim. Her friend. She raised the jar to look inside and found that the little fish, unperturbed, was swimming around inside as if he had lived there all his life.

Back in the apartment, Timothy was placed in a tank of his own. Candida fed him every day, and cleaned out his tank each week. She talked to him, laughed with him, shared secrets with him. Soon, she grew to love him almost as much as she loved Spike. Both these boys were her best friends. Every time she approached Tim's tank, he always swam up to the glass as if to get close to her. When she spoke to him, she was sure he understood. She felt it in her bones.

'When I grow up I'm going to borrow Daddy's bike and ride it all over the world. You'll come with me, Tim?'

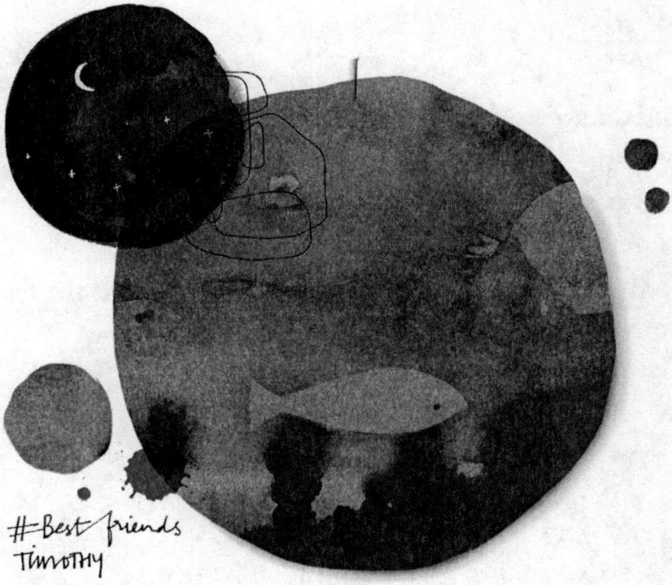

The fish fixed his round, intelligent eye on her. His mouth blew in and out so that little bubbles rose to the surface of the water. It looked as if he was speaking.

'That's a yes, isn't it?' whispered Candida, excitedly.

That night, when it was time for the Louis family's customary bike ride, Candida scooped Tim out of his tank with a long-handled plastic net and dropped him into the glass jar filled with water. 'That's to give you practice for when we travel together!' she laughed and carried him outside to where her parents were waiting.

The four of them sped off. Tim accompanied them every night thereafter.

A year passed. The Louis family saw many changes. Their daughter grew taller, their fish grew longer. Daniel's business took a hit. There were debts to be paid.

'I have the gold coin Grandmama gave us as a wedding gift,' ventured Joanna worriedly one day.

In spite of himself, Daniel smiled and patted the hand that lay on his arm. 'It will take more than that, love. We will have to cut back our expenses now.'

'The ... house ...?'

'No. But ...' he sighed heavily.

'But?' asked Mamma, apprehensively.

'The bike, Jo. I've sold the bike.' His tone was quiet. But not quiet enough to keep Candida, standing with her ear pressed to the dining room door, from overhearing.

Candida felt as if someone had punched her in the stomach. Daddy's words ... no, but he couldn't mean them. They simply didn't make sense. Sell the *bike*? The bike on which they flew together every night? The bike Candida and Tim were to travel the world on? And Timothy. What of Tim? She had taken him out of the temple tank, away from his friends, in the hope of showing him the world.

Now it seemed as if that very world was collapsing around Candida's ears, taking all the joy with it ...

That night, they rode to the Unkal Lake on their last trip together as a family – Mamma, Daddy, Candida and Tim. In the morning the debtor would come to collect the bike. *His* bike. Not Daddy's anymore. On the ride there, Daddy whispered, 'Look at everything passing by so quickly. Do you see it, love?'

Candida, sitting on the petrol tank, clutching the handles with sad, sweaty fingers, nodded numbly. Her father's hands closed gently over hers, warm and reassuring.

'Life is like that, too. We are all just travellers, riding through time, watching as everything passes us by. And everything *is* passing, Candi. Nothing is permanent. Today we are sad, tomorrow that too will pass away.' Candida felt strangely comforted by his words.

As Mamma and Daddy strolled along the path around the Unkal Lake, discussing their future, Candida, holding Tim in his glass jar, went down to the waters. For the very first time, Mamma forgot to call out to her to be careful. At the water's edge, Candida raised the jar and looked at Tim. The fish looked back at her calmly. She unscrewed the lid and, squatting down, tipped the fish into the lake. Tim landed with a tiny splash. He stopped for a heartbeat, as if to get his bearings. And then, with a little quiver of his tail, he darted away. As his friend peered after him, a tear splashed into the water, making it a little bit saltier than it had been before ...

At the roundabout outside the Iyengar Bakery, while summer lightning slashed the night sky in half, Candida Louis got on the motorbike that Spike had stolen from his father's garage, and rode out to Nrupatunga Hill.

She was thirteen years old.

When she reached the hill, she rode past it, and further on ... She went on and on not because she wanted to, but because she hadn't yet learnt how to use the brakes! In fact, her feet barely reached the ground.

When Spike arrived at a curb in the hill an hour later, panting and completely out of breath (having run most of the way), he found the Bullet parked up a tree. That is to say, its front wheel had moulded itself to the trunk, and the handles were wrapped around it like a long-lost friend!

Candida was sitting on a patch of grass nearby, examining her bleeding knuckles with detached interest. Her father's old helmet lay beside her. The black paint had been scratched off in the places that had made contact with the punishing tar road.

'That's the worst parking I have ever seen!' cried Spike, appearing out of the darkness.

'Is it?' asked Candida, looking up at him through her long dark hair. Raindrops ran down the strands and pooled in her lap.

'What were you thinking?' moaned Spike, nearly in tears. His father would have him for breakfast!

'The bike came to the garage for repairs, no?' asked Candida.

'Yes.'

'Good!' said Candida brightly. 'Now there'll be something to repair!'

She dusted off her hands and stood up. They walked to the Bullet together. As they passed under the streetlamp,

Spike exclaimed, 'You're bleeding, Candi! Your face! Your hands—!'

Candida swiftly brushed the cut on her cheek with the sleeve of her t-shirt. 'It's just rainwater,' she mumbled, and busied herself extricating the bike from its verdant embrace.

It was 2:30 in the morning when they wheeled the bike back into Spike's father's garage. Spike had made chalk etchings on the floor to mark where the front and the back wheels had been, so that nobody would notice that the Bullet had ever left the garage. Now, as Candida watched, Spike painstakingly repositioned it, moving it forward and back until the wheels exactly covered the markings. Then, he turned the bent-out-of-shape handles to the angle they had been at the previous evening.

Candida caught up her helmet and waited while Spike spat on the hinges so the garage doors wouldn't creak when he pulled them shut. The worried expression in her best friend's eyes made her feel bad.

'Goodnight, Spike,' she said as she left for home.

'G'night,' he mumbled, pocketing the keys.

After school the next day, Candida returned to the garage, wearing her father's old helmet. (There was nothing unusual about that; she wore it most times except in school, and that only because school rules forbade her from doing so.) She found the garage in an uproar. Nobody could figure out what had happened to the Bullet, and Spike's father was furious and yelling at everybody. This was bad for business! He would have to repair the bike at his own cost and make it look as good as new so the owner would never know what had happened to it.

Spike was sitting huddled in the corner behind a rusted Fiat Padmini, weeping silently. His left cheek looked red. There was the impression of angry fingers stamped upon it. As Candida watched from the entrance, Spike's father marched up to stand over him again.

'You'd better say, Spike! I'm certain you had something to do with this!'

Candida walked up to him. 'Uncle Ronald?' she said.

Spike's father spun around, his eyes popping out of his head in anger.

'It was me,' said Candida calmly. 'I borrowed the bike to learn how to ride it, and I was in an accident. Spike had nothing to do with it. I'm the one who wrecked it. I'm sorry, Uncle Ronald. Here's the money to fix it.'

She put a small wad of notes into his bemused hand and then turned to leave. Ronald looked down at the money in his palm. Vaguely he realized that there was about five thousand rupees there. This brought him to his senses.

'Wait a minute, young lady!' he cried, arresting her mid-step. 'Where did you get the money from? Did you steal it?'

Candida turned around and met his eyes directly, and there was no fear or guilt in her own.

'It's mine,' she said simply, and left.

Back at home, Candida refused the cake her mother had laid out for her tea and went directly to her bedroom. She stood before the mirror and took a deep, deep breath. Slowly she raised her hands and took off the helmet. Her hair was cropped short like a young boy's. She gave a little start. She had not looked in the mirror when the hair dresser had been cutting off her tresses. She had even avoided his eyes when he handed her the five thousand rupees afterwards.

So now, at last, Candida looked at herself. A different person stared back at her from the mirror. For as long as she could remember, she had only ever had long hair. There would be hell to pay when Mamma and Daddy saw her at dinner tonight, but it was worth it. She had ridden a bike all on her own for the very first time in her life, and it had felt like flying! So, she *owed* it to the Bullet and she *owed* it to Spike.

And Candida Louis always paid her dues.

THE STORY OF A RIVER

THE STORY OF A RIVER

Uttar Pradesh

One August morning in 2015, Candida Louis bid goodbye to her parents in Hubballi. It would be a long time before she saw them again. When the four-month vacation from her finance job ended, it would be to Bangalore and work that she returned, and not Hubballi, her home town where her parents continued to live. In the meantime, she meant to travel. To journey alone on her trusty Royal Enfield.

To explore India on a motorcycle ...

From Hubballi, Candida traversed North Karnataka, then headed eastwards to Vishakhapatnam. She explored the beaches of Odisha, visited the Jagannath temple at Puri, and journeyed on to Kolkata, then Siliguri, and, finally, Patna. In those weeks on the road, she had met fellow bikers along the way, who had heard of this intrepid 25-year-old travelling solo through often rough and unfriendly terrain. (In certain parts, like the one Candida was in now, women were rarely seen riding bikes. In fact, women were rarely seen at all!) Full of admiration, those biking enthusiasts usually came to introduce themselves and offer help, should she need it while in their city. Candida was grateful for the kindness of strangers.

After Patna, Candida's next destinations were to be Banaras and Lucknow in the neighbouring state of Uttar Pradesh. News had reached her of a dirt track racing event that was scheduled to be held in Lucknow the following week. Candida was sorely tempted to participate. If only she could make it there in time!

But first, she turned her thoughts to Banaras. Setting out early one morning, Candida found that the Patna-Banaras highway was under repair for most of the way. To her amazement, there were only menfolk everywhere. Womankind seemed to have simply vanished off the face of this part of the earth! Candida raised her hand nervously to the nape of her neck to make sure no stray strands of her long tresses had escaped from beneath the helmet. If people came to know there was a lady under there, it would attract unpleasant attention.

From the practical standpoint, keeping her hair short would have been the far more convenient option while on a journey like this. But after that fateful day in Hubballi twelve years ago, when Candida had sold her hair to repay Spike's father for the bike she had damaged, she had missed the weight of her tresses so desperately that she had never again been able to bring herself to cut her hair. Now it flowed down her back in a straight long sheet (except when bundled under her helmet as it was now!), adding to the feminine grace of her tall, slender figure and beautiful grey eyes.

Five hours into the journey, Candida needed to use a restroom. Now, what to do? She stopped at a wayside restaurant. Men were sitting around smoking bidis and sipping tea. There was not a woman in sight. Keeping her helmet on, Candida took a deep breath, squared her shoulders and strode briskly inside. When she emerged from the restroom a few minutes later, an abrupt hush fell over the place. Had these people realized that she was female? Or had the unusual sight of the biker's jacket, helmet, gloves and boots been the reason for their sudden silence? She could feel all eyes boring into her as she walked towards the front entrance. She kept her pace casual and deliberate, even though her instincts were screaming, 'RUN'!

'Ay sahib, chai nahin peeni hai, kya?' called the owner. *Sahib*! They thought she was a man, then, thank god! But they wouldn't think that for long if she stuck around for a cup of tea. Without turning, Candida refused the man's offer with a casual wave of her gloved hand, and exited through the front door. Swiftly mounting the Royal Enfield, she sped away. Her heart raced and sweat continued to trickle down her back almost until the next village, five kilometres away!

When she was an hour's ride from Banaras, the ambience began to change. Women could be seen from time to time, and then, all of a sudden, there were chariots. Wait a minute, *chariots*?? What were chariots doing on the road in the 21st century? And not one or two, but twenty, thirty of them! Gaudily decorated with flowers, streamers and flashing lights, and accompanied by groups of festively dressed people on foot, they inched along the highway causing quite a traffic jam. Enthroned upon these chariots were newly married couples – grooms in turbans and sherwanis, brides with faces hidden behind ghoonghats, dripping with jewellery. It was wedding season in Banaras! Candida soon discovered that they were heading to various open grounds along the way, where the wedding receptions were to be held.

She passed one such ground, decorated with shamianas. Beside the dais where the hapless bride and groom sat, a podium had been erected. Behind it stood a stalwart with a large moustache and turban, making announcements over a loudspeaker. Fascinated, Candida parked her bike on the side of the road and watched. Before her amazed eyes, wedding guests stepped up one by one and handed the stalwart their gift envelopes. These, the man proceeded to open and check. After each he leaned forward and shouted into the mike, 'Chandrachur Singh, two hundred rupees! Om Prakash Singh, five hundred rupees! Dharamveer Singh, EMPTY PACKET!!'

Poor Dharamveer Singh slinked away amidst boos from the crowd. Chuckling to herself, Candida started the bike and went on her way.

Banaras. Varanasi. Kashi. They called it the City of Life. Candida entered the city limits by late afternoon and found that it was, on the contrary, the City of Death. Frequently along the way to the guesthouse, she encountered funeral processions, heading for ... where she wasn't sure.

I don't think I'm going to like it here, thought Candida with a shudder. After a fifteen-minute ride through narrow, teeming alleyways, she arrived at the guesthouse that some biker friends had recommended. It was a quaint little place, small, basic and inexpensive. All its charm lay in the old couple who ran it – a husband and wife whose twinkling eyes and ready laughter seemed not to have forgotten what it was like to be young. They spoke five foreign languages, which the old man assured her they had learnt over the years from their 'imported guests', and not from any language school!

'Mi esposa es mejor que yo en lenguas internacionales, hija,' he whispered conspiratorially to her in Spanish. 'I'm just a better actor, that's all!' He threw back his head and laughed at Candida's incomprehension. 'I said, "My wife is better at foreign languages than I am, beti, but I'm a better actor so nobody can tell the difference!"' he exclaimed. His laughter was so infectious that Candida found herself joining in.

I think I'm going to like Banaras, after all, she thought to herself. With the old man's admonition (this time in Portuguese!) to use the geyser ringing in her ear, she went to her room to take a shower. Later, she returned downstairs and asked the couple what she should do next.

'Go visit the university and Lallapura where the Muslim weavers weave Banaras silk saris. Then visit the ghats,' advised the old man. 'If you go to Dashaswamedh at sunset, you'll catch Ganga arti.'

'What's Ganga arti?' asked Candida curiously.

'Find out for yourself,' he replied with mock sternness, and his wife smiled mysteriously. They refused to say any more, so Candida set out on the Royal Enfield. Her first stop was the famous Banaras Hindu University.

Founded in 1916, BHU is the largest residential institution in all of Asia. Candida stared at its majestic buildings and grounds, so well-maintained, and wondered why the rest of Banaras was so unkempt. She took her time exploring the campus, feeling the sheer historical weight of the place. The 1,300 acres across which it was spread had been donated by the erstwhile raja of Banaras. The South Campus, she was assured, was twice the size. Candida wished she could get a bird's eye view of the place. That would be pretty awesome! Slowly, she wandered away from the buildings and back to where her bike was parked.

The busy, rhythmic clatter of hundreds of handlooms told Candida that she had arrived in the locality of Lallapura. This was the home of the Banaras silk sari, the womb in which skilful hands meticulously wove warp and weft to conceive exquisitely ornate fabric. Silk threads of splendid hues, along with silver and gold, all came together in the hands of the Muslim artisans to culminate in the world-famous Banaras silk, worn from the era of Mughal royalty until this, the modern day. Mass-production had still not infiltrated the world of the weavers, who painstakingly crafted each sari by hand, over weeks and sometimes even months.

Candida was struck by how low the light was in those karkhaanas, the workshops that dominated the streets of Lallapura. She also observed that while the overriding personality of Banaras was Hindu, a pocket of the city like this one was dominated by green—the colour of Islam—from the flags fluttering from electric poles down to the motifs on the saris, and the hands that made them. It seemed strange that regardless of the claims of a politically motivated outside world, places like this existed, quietly and inextricably amalgamating history, cultures and religions into the essence of this city that was believed to be as old as Time.

From Lallapura, Candida headed to the ghats. She picked one from the list that Google had painstakingly enumerated. Assi Ghat, in the southern-most part of the city, was the closest to the BHU campus, and promised to be more quietly bustling than the rest. Here, the Assi river met the Ganga. Pilgrims came to dip themselves in the holy river before worshipping Lord Shiva in the form of a large lingam installed under a pipal tree nearby. Candida made her way to the spot where the steps descended right into the waters, and for the first time saw with her own eyes what a 'ghat' was. Despite the activity around her, there was silence. She sat for a long time, watching the murky waters of the Ganga flowing past, and letting the peace of the place sink in. Suddenly, her phone rang. It was a group of bikers in the city who wanted to meet her.

'Sure. Tell me where?' asked Candida.

'Can you come to Dashaswamedh Ghat at 6.45 p.m., ma'am?' asked the biker. 'We'll be waiting for you there.'

Candida still had several hours in hand before the appointed time, and so she visited Tulsi Ghat (where the famous poet saint Tulsidas had written part of his

Ramacharitamanas), Chet Singh Ghat, and the beautiful observatory at Man Mandir Ghat. Then, she began exploring the streets of Banaras on foot. Walking through the alleyways of this city was an experience in itself. Many a time, Candida found herself leaping out of the way of a speeding motorcycle or hurriedly pressing up against a wall to give way to crowds of people, wandering cows, and, once, even a galloping buffalo calf that seemed to be in a hurry to get someplace! The streets were dotted with tiny temples, clothes stores, shops that sold cooking vessels, tea, snacks, mithai, and just about everything else under the sun. Banaras silk saris appeared in many a store window, and Candida paused to admire the resplendent, intricate designs and the stark silver zari that stood out against brilliant backgrounds of silk. Every establishment was named after the lords Rama, Krishna, or, most often, Shiva. Lord Shiva seemed to be a popular figure around there.

Candida glanced at her watch. 6.35 p.m. She slowly backtracked to Dashaswamedh Ghat, which was not far away. There, she found the bikers eagerly waiting for her. They shook hands enthusiastically all around, and she was happy to see a girl in their midst. The ghat was fast filling up with people. Suddenly, just as the sun sank into the western horizon, the sound of conches filled the air, sending a thrill through Candida. The sound went on and on. A row of priests stood upon pedestals facing the Ganga flowing past the steps of the ghat. They were dressed alike, in long shirts and dhotis.

Drum beats, sacred chants and bhajans began, while the priests, ringing brass bells, twirled first incense sticks, then smoky loban in ever-widening circles, in honour of the river. Finally, they raised majestic, hand-held brass stands with layer upon layer of dancing flames, and began to swing them around in slow circles. They raised, lowered and dipped them, then changed hands to swing them back the other way, all in tandem. This was mankind's nightly tribute to the mighty river, the regular worship of which was believed to guarantee them salvation from the endless cycle of birth and death.

The Eternal Sleep

Candida was spellbound! She had never experienced anything like this before. So this was why the old couple had refused to explain to her what Ganga arti was. There were no words to describe the beauty of the ritual – they had wanted her to experience it for herself.

'Ma'am?' came one of the biker's voices. 'The arti is finished. Hum khaana khane chalein, kya?'

Candida glanced at her watch. Nearly 7.30 p.m.. Forty-five minutes! She had been so mesmerized she didn't realize the arti had gone on for that long. She looked up at her new friends and found them watching her expectantly. 'Hmm?' she murmured vaguely.

'Dinner, ma'am?' asked Rithika, the female biker. Candida nodded. She followed the others quietly up the ghat steps. Suddenly Rithika put a hand on Candida's arm and said softly, 'Hota hai, ma'am. It is always like this when you witness Ganga arti. It leaves you feeling awed. Aur yeh apka first time tha, na ma'am?'

Candida smiled at the girl. In companionable silence, they walked to the bikes.

They ate a simple vegetarian dinner, as no meat was served in restaurants around the ghat area. Then, navigating their way deftly through crowded lanes, tooting their horns incessantly to clear a path for themselves through the throng of humankind and 'cowkind', they took Candida to a fantastic place that was practically an institution in Banaras – a lassi shop! Lassi, or sweet buttermilk, was served fresh and hand-churned here. The family that owned the place had been churning out buttermilk for the public for close to a hundred and twenty-five years, and had never once used a beater or a blender to do so! They had no intentions of starting now. Their menu boasted *one hundred and ten* different varieties of lassi in all permutations and combinations! The shop went by the unremarkable name of Blue Lassi Shop, and was little more than an unprepossessing hole-in-the-blue-wall (for the store front was painted a cheerful blue that accounted for its name). Candida would scarcely have guessed that it was one of the most famous lassi shops in India. But ten minutes later, when she wrapped her hands around the earthen container and took her first taste of the coconut-chocolate-blueberry flavoured beverage, she understood exactly why it had earned such a reputation for itself! The drink was absolutely delicious – thick, creamy and flavourful, garnished with chocolate shavings and blueberries, making it as much a treat for the eye as for the tongue.

From the spiritual heights evoked by Ganga arti, Candida felt herself come crashing down to the earthly pleasures of a good dessert ... and smile contentedly as she did so! Sweet Banarasi paan, prepared by the skilful hands of an old paan seller, completed the experience.

The next morning, on Rithika's recommendation, Candida rose early and took a boat ride along the ghats. It was still dark outside; only the faintest blush stained the eastern sky. Sailing down the Ganga, Candida caught glimpses of individual ghats as they went by. Each was distinctive and beautiful, dotted with temples and shops, and occasionally a minaret in the distance. Even at this pre-dawn hour, people had come to bathe in the river, salute the rising sun ... and wash their clothes! Lulled by the gentle motion of the boat and the rhythmic creak of the oars, Candida felt herself slip into a trance as she watched the bustling activity on the banks (the sounds of which reached her across the water). They were floating past Scindia Ghat now, and she saw a temple partially submerged in the river. The boatman informed her that it was a Shiva temple that had collapsed under its own weight.

'It is still sinking, memsahib,' the old man, who was named Mohammed Pasha, said. 'One day it will completely vanish under water, phushhh!' He flashed a toothless smile, and she couldn't help warming to him. So old, and yet he pulled at the oars so tirelessly. Now they had crossed Scindia Ghat, and a strange haze of smoke seemed to hang over the next one.

'Is something burning, Mohammed Chacha?' asked Candida curiously, straining to make out what was behind all the smoke.

The old man smiled again, but this time it was a strange smile, no longer cheerful. 'People,' he informed her quietly, and she gave a start.

'It is the Hindu burning ghat, memsahib.'

Candida was taken aback. 'At *this* time of the day?'

'At *all* times of the day. And night. Fires here have not stopped burning for hundreds of years. Not even for a minute.'

They had come abreast of the ghat now. The name painted on the wall read: Manikarnika Ghat. The ghat steps were piled high with wooden logs, as were the buildings beyond. People sat around watching the fires at play.

The boat was still. The boatman had drawn in his oars and was watching the sight on the banks silently. Candida did not like lingering here. She wanted to tell him to row on, but she couldn't find her voice. Then he said, 'The Hindus believe that Lord Shiva himself will come to this place and take the souls of the dead. They will never again have to incarnate in this world. No more death ...' He spoke with a sort of yearning, this old, old man. Suddenly, he turned and looked at her, a happy smile chasing away the sadness from his eyes. 'That's why everybody wants to come to Banaras to die! So simple, no?' he laughed.

He started rowing again, and they pulled away from Manikarnika. Candida turned to look at it one last time. She saw fires and smoke, and logs of wood. She saw people sitting there and watching the pyres. At first, she had thought that this was life witnessing death. But she had been wrong. In Banaras, there was no death. There was only Life witnessing the passing of life. The first ray of the sun peeped over the horizon and fell upon the still waters of the Ganga and all the people on it.

'Banaras,' whispered Candida softly to herself. 'City of Life ...'

A six-hour ride from Banaras had brought Candida to Lucknow, in time for the dirt track race. The dirt track was a riot! Hundreds of people had turned up to watch the riders take their chances with the sand and the stones beneath their wheels, with the dust that flew into their eyes and clogged their noses and their chances of completing the race!

'I thought this was a race against other people,' Candida told a press reporter who came to take her interview for the *Dainik Jagran* afterwards. 'It turned out to be a race against myself!'

The reporter, Devaki, glanced down and saw Candida's bandaged right palm. 'You hurt yourself, ma'am?' she asked, immediately concerned.

'Just a scratch,' said Candida, carelessly. This was, after all, the same girl who had rammed into a tree the first time she had ridden a bike at the age of thirteen. She shared that story with Devaki, who listened agog.

'*Purposely* you rammed into a tree? But why??'

'Didn't know where the brakes were. There was no other way to stop!' Candida replied, laughing.

'And this time what happened?' asked Devaki, indicating Candida's injured hand.

'There were about ten guys out there on the track. Sheena and I were the only two women riders. She kept close to me. I was riding a Royal Enfield Thunderbird, and Sheena was on a KTM Duke. Both bikes are heavy, not easy to manage and manoeuvre on such a rugged track, which was more of an obstacle course than anything else. Anyway, at one point Sheena completely lost control of her bike. She fell directly in the path of my front wheel. I swerved sharply to avoid running over her and I too lost my balance and fell. Must have cut my palm on a stone at that point, I'm not sure.'

'Did you win, ma'am?' asked the reporter.

'Most of us did,' replied Candida.

'Yeh kaise ho sakta hai, ma'am? How could *most* of you win? Winner toh ek hi hota hai, na?' There can only be one winner, right?

'Like I said, it was a race between the riders and their own selves. Anyone who finished the race was a winner! Except for four riders, the rest of us completed the course, so we all received prizes at the end.'

'What were the prizes?' asked the reporter. Her eyes were on her note pad, where she was furiously scribbling down everything Candida was saying, but in Hindi; *Dainik Jagran* was a Hindi newspaper.

'Everyone got a different one. Mine is money – seven thousand five hundred bucks! I'm thrilled!' exclaimed Candida.

'There was nothing else you would have liked as a prize?'

'I'm riding across India on a very tight budget, because I don't have a sponsor. So, every penny counts. This money will be a big help.'

The reporter looked up here and smiled. 'Do you like Lucknow, ma'am?'

In Candida's mind flashed beautiful old monuments with stately lines and swooping arches, and the music in the everyday Urdu of the people. Their gracious manners—tehzeeb, the Lucknowis called it—was a throwback from the era of the Nawabs who had once patronized this city. On Candida's tongue lingered the richness of the Awadhi food that was a legacy of the Mughal kitchens, the kebabs and the kormas she had eaten in those past few days ...

'I love it,' she said simply, with her heart in her eyes. 'I'm staying with a wonderful family—the Chauhans—who are relatives of a biker friend. In four short days, they have become like family to me. We've been exploring the city together. We visited Aminabad Bazaar—'

'Did you eat at Tunday Kababi there?'

'Of course. And I made sure to order the tundey kababs!' laughed Candida, . 'I figured that if they've named the restaurant after a dish then they must make that dish really well, you know what I mean?'

'And did they?' asked the journalist with a twinkle in her eye.

'I have never tasted anything so delicious in my life!' sighed Candida.

'The recipe for tundey kabab is hundred years old, ma'am, maloom hai apko?'

'Well, now that you've told me, I know! So we ate lots of fantastic food, we shopped till we dropped—'

'Chikankaari kurtas?'

'Two sets! And I don't even wear kurtas much, I'm usually always in biking gear. It's just that when I saw all those beautiful outfits at Aminabad bazaar, I couldn't resist! We visited Chowk, Hazratganj bazaar and Yahiyaganj market as well, just to get a feel of the city. I left my wallet behind at home on purpose, just so I wouldn't bankrupt myself! My god, the Lucknowis must be shopaholics with all the bazaars there are around here!'

'Our bazaars are very famous, ma'am,' smiled Devaki.

'On the second day we visited Chota Imambara. It was so beautiful, almost pristine. Then from there we headed out to Bhool Bhulaiyya. It was really exciting and also a little scary.'

'Why scary? You got lost?'

'Of course we got lost,' chuckled Candida. 'That's the whole point of that place, isn't it? We got so lost in some of the dark chambers that the guide had to come and rescue us! I wonder how he finds his way around. Google Maps?' she joked with a wink.

'What is the thing you like best about Lucknow?'

Candida's eyes softened. 'Mrs Chauhan,' she said. 'She's become like a mother to me.'

'And from here, ma'am? Where will you go from here?' asked Devaki.

Candida smile faded and her eyes took on a faraway look. 'North,' she said softly. 'North, to the Himalayas ...'

INTO THE MOON LAKE

INTO THE MOON LAKE

Chandra Tal

The road through the Spiti Valley of Himachal Pradesh was terribly beautiful. Terrible. Beautiful. Both.

Candida Louis had left Shimla five days ago and ridden through Narkanda, then traversed the Jeori Pass to get to that secret place few ever visited ... Chandra Tal.

The Moon Lake.

'Chandra Tal: 3 km' the milestone read. Candida's heart quickened! The Royal Enfield was wobbling from side to side almost as much as it was moving forward. It reminded Candida of her childhood, so many years ago, when Daddy had first let her manage the bike handles all by herself. The bike beneath her had wobbled then as it was wobbling now, on this lonely dirt road. Only, *then* she had been an eleven-year-old child, and it had been her first time. And now? Now she was a twenty-four-year-old woman, an expert biker who ran her own biking agency, making her way across India on a motorcycle. Alone.

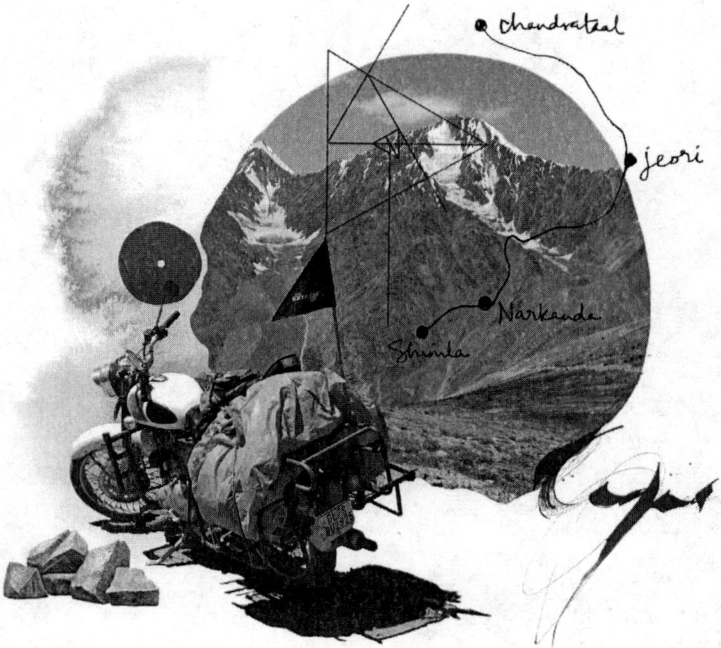

The road to Chandra Tal was little more than a mud track with stones and rocks. It had been this way for miles and miles. The valley, robed in azure skies, and snow-capped mountains adorning it like strings of jasmines, seemed to have glimpsed its reflection in the passing lakes and shrugged thinking, *If people come to visit me, let them sleep under the stars. I will wrap them in my blanket of sky, and they may drink from my waters. No need for tar roads and other such pointless human luxuries!*

'Chandra Tal: 2 km', the milestone now read.

Against her better judgement, Candida speeded up. Her eagerness to see the Moon Lake was like the proverbial shot in her tired arms, grown painful from struggling to hold the bike handles steady. The Royal Enfield was teetering dangerously, but she barely noticed anymore, for she had passed yet another sign that declared: 'Chandra Tal: 500 metres'.

Candida closed her eyes and some other force took over. It was as if the Royal Enfield was carrying her to her destination of its own accord. She never knew when she applied the brakes and cut off the engine with a twist of the key. She only knew that the Royal Enfield was no longer in motion, and that there was ground beneath her feet. She staggered the last remaining steps of the way until she came to a stop with a sense of space—endless space—stretching out before her. And she *felt* before she *knew* that she had arrived at last. She opened her eyes, slowly ...

Chandra Tal.

There it was! That boundless blue lake, those mountains standing on their snow-capped heads. Mountains ... standing *upside down* ... on their snow-capped *heads*? Wait a minute. That couldn't be right. She gasped and stared. It was an illusion! The lake was so clear that the mountains were perfectly mirrored in waters that were utterly unmoving, utterly still. Waters that appeared almost solid to the touch. It was impossible to tell which was the reflection and which the real thing.

Mesmerized, Candida moved forward. Accustomed to the greyish waters of the Unkal Lake, and the restless writhing of its opaque body against the embankments back home in Hubballi, to her Chandra Tal seemed ethereal.

'Here,' she thought with a stab of regret, 'in this beautiful place, is where I might have released Tim. This should have been his home.'

The Moon Lake was calling out to her now, and she broke into a run, closing the distance between herself and its waters, plunging straight into its loving embrace. The solid stillness of its glassy surface juddered and cracked, making way for her, closing around her, filling her boots, her jacket, creeping beneath her helmet to wind itself into the thick strands of her hair. It filled her heart with its icy fire.

Suddenly, she realized it was freezing hot. Or burning cold. She couldn't tell which. She turned her face up to the sky in joy. Her body was trembling violently but she barely knew it. Tears ran down her face and dropped into the lake like raindrops from a friendly, passing cloud. As she had done to Unkal so many years ago, she added a touch of salt to waters that had known only sweetness this far.

'HAVE YOU GONE *CRAZY*??' bellowed a voice, cutting through her reverie and bringing her sharply back to her senses.

Spike! thought Candida for one dazed second.

'Come out of there, NOW!' commanded the voice.

She pushed the hair out of her eyes and turned to see a young man standing on the bank of the lake, gesturing wildly to her. Behind him were two others, looking as agitated as their companion sounded. Candida realized that something was badly wrong. As quickly as her soaking attire and water-filled boots would let her, she waded back to the shore.

'Where are your things?' the men demanded. 'You must change out of those wet clothes at once!'

Candida was shivering uncontrollably now. Her lips had turned blue.

'Jatin! That's her bike there, I think. Get her stuff. Hurry!' called the first guy.

Meanwhile, he made Candida sit down upon a patch of grass. The fellow named Jatin returned a minute later looking worried.

'There's nothing on the back of her bike, Chetan.'

Chetan frowned and turned to Candida. 'You came without luggage?' he asked, incredulously.

Candida slouched forward, hugging herself tightly. She shouldn't have speeded up on that dirt road!

'It ... m...must ... have ... f...fallen ... off ... al ... along ... the ... w...way,' she gasped.

Chetan moved fast. 'Guys, take whatever you can from my haversack and get her to put them on. I'm going off to see if I can find her stuff.'

When Candida was dry again, Jatin pulled his leather jacket over her shoulders, and the third guy, Rahul, thrust a thermos of hot tea into her hands. She sipped gratefully under their vigilant eyes.

'They are looking at me like I'm some species of weird, tea-drinking-bug-under-a-microscope,' she thought to herself, and began to giggle uncontrollably. She didn't know it then, but the giggling was part of her body's mechanism to generate some much-needed heat, and it probably saved her life. The men watched her in silence until the giggling subsided.

'Did you think it was a hot spring?' enquired Rahul, politely. Candida looked up at him and blinked. Suddenly she burst out laughing all over again. This time Rahul's mouth twitched. There was an unmistakable twinkle in his eye. He glanced at Jatin, who grinned outright.

When Chetan returned with a very dusty haversack that bore the initials 'C.L.', he found his friends and the 'stupid girl' (as he referred to her in his head) rolling with laughter on the banks of the Chandra Tal. After a bit, Candida sat up and wiped the tears from her eyes. 'I can't resist water,' she explained. 'Once I jumped into a dam and swam in its waters for half an hour. When I got out I saw a sign that said: "Beware of Crocodiles. Survivors Will Be Prosecuted."'

'Is this yours?' asked Chetan drily, holding out the haversack.

'Oh, yes! Thank you!' she cried, leaping to her feet and taking the haversack into her arms. Then she looked around as if searching for something. 'Er ... you didn't happen to find a sleeping bag, did you?' she asked hopefully.

'Nope.'

'Okay,' said Candida matter-of-factly and shrugged. 'Serves me right, I guess,' she added, under her breath. The loss of her sleeping bag on a journey like this was a huge blow. But it was not the time to think about that just now.

'Where've you come from?' asked Jatin.

'Hubballi. It's in Karnataka,' replied Candida.

Chetan nodded. 'We know where Hubballi is,' he said.

'Do you? That's nice. Most people in the North refer to South Indians across the board as "Madraasis". By the way, my name is Candida Louis.'

'You don't say,' said Rahul with a grin. 'I thought the initials on your knapsack stood for "Crazy Lady". Do you know you could have died out there in those waters?'

'But I didn't!' replied Candida, grinning cheerfully up at him. 'Thanks to you guys! My dad says I'll survive my own death.'

'I hope so. Well, we'd better be off. See you, Candida. Take care of yourself.'

After shaking hands with her new friends, she sat down on the banks of Chandra Tal, still clutching the haversack to her for warmth. And there she sat until the pinkish glow in the eastern sky bruised to purple, and finally turned black. When the darkness finally swallowed up the lake and its surrounding mountains, Candida got up and left.

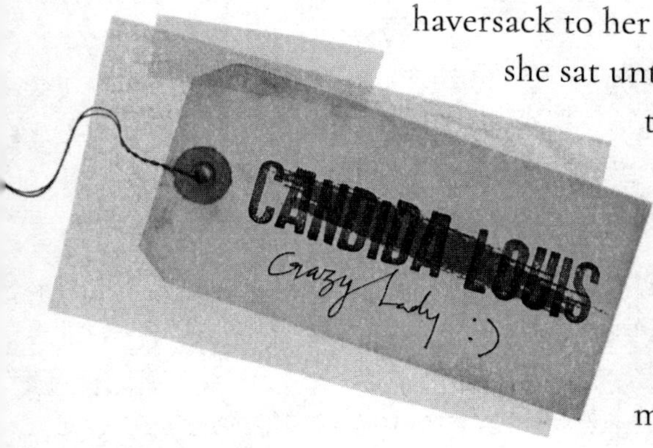

It's a good thing Tim remained in Hubballi, she thought with a shiver as she mounted her bike. *He wouldn't have been able to stand such cold waters.*

She looked about her one last time and saw that the moon had crept into the lake and was swimming in it. 'Chandra Tal,' she whispered and her heart stood still at the sight of it. 'Moon Lake ...'

Candida stayed the night in the hut of a shepherd, in the nearby village of Pangmo. The old man and his wife spoke only broken Hindi, but they were very kind and received her warmly when she came asking for a place to sleep. They had a little granddaughter who lived with them, a lovely child with sun-bleached hair and rosy cheeks. They called her Afsar Ara, by her full name, and whenever they did, she stopped playing and looked at them silently from the corner of her tip-tilted eyes.

'Her mother is dead,' the shepherd's wife informed Candida quietly as they sat together by the fire in the front yard of the house, while the old lady cooked. 'But we told her that she has gone to the city to work.'

Candida watched the child as she played with her doll. She tried to make friends, but the child was shy. The family was very poor, as were the smattering of other families that made up the village. The shepherd had this hut and little else, yet there sat his wife, cooking mutton soup for her guest over the kitchen fire. Candida opened her knapsack and pulled out a packet of MTR ready-to-eat tamarind rice. She quickly prepared it and added it to the meal laid out. As they sat around the fire eating dinner, she saw Afsar Ara hesitate over the tamarind rice in her tin plate. She had never seen anything like it before. She put a bit in her mouth and frowned. The flavour was new on her tongue. She quickly gulped down some soup. Then she reached again for the tamarind rice and her eyes darted to their guest. Candida looked away at once. The child picked up more rice and ate it. Soon it was all gone. After a third helping, when her plate had been cleared away, the little girl sat in the corner by herself licking the lingering tanginess off her fingers. Finally, with childlike nonchalance she wiped her hands on her grubby woollen over-robe, and went to bed.

The shepherd insisted on giving Candida his place in the tiny hut, but she would not hear of it. So he replenished the fire in the front yard for her and handed her a blanket. Candida huddled close to the flames, soaking up their warmth. She looked up at the stars in the velvety night sky and the moon that had risen in it.

'This is the same moon that swims in Chandra Tal,' she mused drowsily. 'The same moon that Mamma and Daddy must be looking up at in Hubballi. We are all connected, then. Nobody is ever really far away ...' Lulled by that thought, Candida drifted off to sleep.

Around midnight, the fire died out. It was freezing cold. Without her sleeping bag, Candida was in a bad way. Shivering, she fumbled inside her haversack and removed all the clothes she had in there. She wore them all, one over the other, then pulled on her helmet. Much better! Gradually the shivering stopped. Tired out, she fell back to sleep again.

The next morning, Candida was roused by the peals of childish laughter. The shepherd's granddaughter, Afsar Ara, had come out of the hut and spotted the funny guest asleep in a helmet. Thrilled, she had summoned all her little friends in the village to come and witness the sight. Candida sat up and grinned at the pink-cheeked children standing around her. They started to run away, but she held out her hand and they hesitated. Then one by one they came forward and shook it solemnly. Clearly, to them this was a ceremony of some sort. When it was Afsar Ara's turn, Candida smiled at her. A shy, answering smile touched the child's lips as she turned away.

After breakfast, Candida packed her belongings and pulled on her leather jacket that had recovered nicely from its excursion in the lake the previous afternoon. Then, she took the shepherd aside and offered him money for letting her stay with them. The old man was mortified! He protested, waggling his hands animatedly to convey his refusal. He spoke rapidly in his own tongue, but the only words Candida could understand were, 'Allah baksh!'

Gift from God. He considered all things a gift from God. His kindness, the food from his table, the warmth of his home and the fire he had built for her, all were gifts from God. How, then, could he charge her money for it? Candida had no words to thank him. Instead, she went inside and embraced the old lady in farewell. From her knapsack, she removed the remaining packets of ready-to-eat tamarind rice and slipped them under Afsar Ara's sleeping mat. She had no more food left with her, but that did not matter.

Someone up there will provide when I need it, she thought, as she rode away from Pangmo on her Royal Enfield.
Allah baksh ...

WIND IN THE MOUNTAINS

WIND IN THE MOUNTAINS

Kashmir – Part 1

In the time of Emperor Akbar, there lived a girl in a valley, who grew up among saffron fields, and played in the shade of the Chinar. Lovely as the moon, she married Yusuf Shah Chak, king of Kashmir. But soon, too soon, the lovers were forced to part. The Emperor invited Chak to Delhi and, there, imprisoned him by stealth. Broken-hearted, the queen wandered through the valley of Gurais, searching for her lover among the mountains, knowing well that he was not there. When news of his death reached her, she renounced the world and spent her days singing poems of love and loss. The mountains heard her song and wept. Their tears gushed forth in torrents ... and River Krishanganga was born.

So says the legend of Habba Khatoon.

On the left fork, lay Baramulla. On the right, Kargil. Candida Louis took the middle road that led straight on to Bandipora. For, just a little beyond it lay Gurais ...

The legend of Habba Khatoon had lured Candida to a valley that dwelt among snow-covered mountains, some 8000 feet above the sea. When she heard the story from the film crew in Leh, she knew that it was time to pack her bags again.

'The journey will be tough,' Ranjit, the crew's cameraman had told her. 'But then ...' and he had broken off with a smile and a shrug. Candida had understood him perfectly. The difficult journeys were often the most compelling, because of what one might find at the end of them.

After a chance meeting the previous week with this film crew at Hemis—a Buddhist gompa in Ladakh, not far from the capital city of Leh—a friendship had sprung up between them. Fascinated by the idea of a young lady biking it solo across the country, they had gathered around and bombarded her with enthusiastic questions. Laughing, she had not managed to answer half of them before it was time for the monastery to close to visitors for the day.

'Let's meet again!' Sonia, the host of the travel show had cried. 'You're staying in Leh, aren't you?'

'No, wait! I have a better idea,' Anupama had piped in. 'Why don't you explore Ladakh with us?'

Candida had been only too happy to comply. Over the next few days, they had covered many places, filming across the region extensively. They had ridden (with some difficulty, due to the lack of oxygen at an altitude of 18,380 feet!) to Khardung La, the highest motorable road in the world. They had even explored the villages around it. (A village, it turned out, in such punishing terrain, was usually made up of two huts, three-and-a-half people, and a goat!) The crew had gone on to explore the gompa at Thikse, returned to Hemis twice, descended into the Nubra Valley, and travelled to Pangong Tso.

As they approached Pangong, Candida had raised the windscreen on her helmet and called to Ranjit and Sonia, 'When we get to the lake, don't let me jump in!'

Ranjit had raised his eyebrows in surprise, and Candida laughed. 'I can't resist water. I nearly froze to death in Chandra Tal! I'm kind of stupid that way.'

Sonia had spent enough time with Candida by now to know that she was perfectly capable of doing something like that. So, when they reached the head of Pangong Lake, Sonia had grabbed hold of the tail of Candida's jacket until she was certain that the euphoria of Candida's first glimpse of the lake had worn off. And well might she have. For, Pangong Tso was the most stunning sight! Clusters of hills—pink, purple, grey, brown and red—stood grouped around the waters to the backdrop of a blemishless blue sky. The bottom of the lake was scattered with a collage of mosaics and colourful stones, and the crystal-clear waters afforded such an uninterrupted view of the bed that one could have mistaken it for being shallow. And if that person happened to be Candida Louis, well, she might even have jumped in!

They stayed the night in tents by Pangong, and returned to Leh the following day. All of Ladakh was beautiful, no doubt. But, by far, the sight of the muddy brown Ladakh River merging with the azure waters of the Zanskar at the base of the ravine just beyond Magnetic Hill had been the most enthralling to Candida. It was a sight she would never forget.

Over seven days, the film crew (with Candida in tow) had covered as much as it had hoped to of the Ladakh region for its travel show. On the morning of the eighth day, its members were to leave for Srinagar. Candida was to remain in Leh for another week, then make her way southwest through Amritsar, on to Rajasthan.

Fate decreed otherwise.

The night before the crew's departure, they had sat around a bonfire eating thukpa and momos. Ranjit, staring into the flames of the fire, had spoken the legend of Habba Khatoon in an unknown tongue to himself. It was only because Candida had been sitting close by that she had heard.

'What was that?' she asked curiously. 'What did you just say, Ranjit?'

Ranjit had looked up, startled. 'Nothing.'

'No, you said something. What language was it in?'

'Kashmiri, probably.' It was Sonia who spoke. Candida turned her head quickly.

'He speaks *Kashmiri*?'

'He *is* Kashmiri,' Sonia had smiled. 'Kashmiri Pandit. His surname is Kaul.'

Turning back to Ranjit excitedly, Candida had burst out, 'So you live in—'

'Delhi,' Ranjit had interposed curtly. 'I live in Delhi. My family left Srinagar when I was 16.'

'Tell me what it is that you were saying just now by the fire, na? Please?'

There was a long silence. The others had gathered closer to listen. Then, Ranjit had spoken in a lilting voice lines that seemed both poetry and song:

'*In the time of Emperor Akbar, there lived a girl in a valley, who grew up among saffron fields and played in the shade of the Chinar ...*'

Thus, Ranjit Kaul had told the story of the famous poet saint of Kashmir, Habba Khatoon, only this time in English. And at that moment, Candida knew in her heart that Gurais was calling out to her. Without another thought, she decided to cut short her stay in Ladakh and leave with the crew for Srinagar in the morning. From there she would journey on alone for another 123 kilometres, into the valley of Gurais.

Now here she was, riding along the dirt roads that would take her to Bandipora alongside the tour guide that Ranjit had organized for her in Srinagar. The guide, Motilal, had arranged for all the necessary permits that would get her past the army check posts that dotted the area and sprung up every few kilometres. Militancy was a serious threat in these parts, and the army couldn't afford to take any chances.

They arrived in Bandipora the same afternoon. Motilal took her directly to Heevan Guest House (had they meant 'Heaven' Guest House?) and settled her in. When the check-in formalities were over, he turned to Candida with a smile to tell her he was leaving. 'Main chalta hoon, madam. From here, only eighty-six kilometres to Gurais. Aap ja sakti hai yahan se, no problem. Leave in morning, better. Road not good, slowly-slowly you will have to go, will take some long time.'

'Don't worry about me, Motilalji, I'll be fine. Won't you have lunch before you head back?'

'No madam. Must reach Sri before dark is becoming.'

She thanked him for his help, and walked with him to the entrance of the hotel, where he got on his Bullet and rode away. After a quick bath, Candida decided to go out and explore the area a little. The Royal Enfield had withstood those punishing dirt roads admirably, for which she was grateful. There was hardly any network in these parts, but an STD booth would allow her to call her parents, whom she hadn't spoken to in three days, and who must certainly be worrying about her.

So, after a visit to the Wular Lake, on whose banks Bandipora was situated, she asked around until someone pointed her to an STD booth. The booth was dusty and isolated. There were very few people in sight. Ducking inside the narrow cubicle, Candida dialled the Hubballi code and then her home telephone number. She didn't want to call either of her parents on their cell phones, for fear that the number would show up on their display screen. It would never do for them to know she was in Kashmir, because it would frighten them unnecessarily.

A sense of wellbeing flowed through her at the sound of her mother's voice. Candida reassured Joanna that she was fine, and told her all about Leh, speaking as if she were still there.

'Mamma, it will be a while before I can call again, a few days at least. The networks here are terrible.'

'But Candi, is it safe, darling?' asked her mother anxiously.

'Very safe, Mamma. Don't worry.'

After she hung up the phone, Candida lingered in the booth for a little while longer, crying briefly before pulling herself together and wiping her eyes. It had been over two months since she had seen her parents, and she missed them terribly. She had never been away from them for this long before. Only, the pull of adventure had been strong, so strong ...

Putting on her helmet, she stepped out of the booth. Just as she was paying for the call, an army convoy passed that way. The officer in the first vehicle caught sight of her and stared in surprise. He waved the driver to a halt. The other trucks coming up behind pulled up as well, slightly alarmed by the unscheduled stop. Undoing the catch on his holster as a precaution, the officer jumped down from the truck and approached. Seeing the booth keeper's gaze riveted fearfully on some object behind her right shoulder, Candida turned quickly. She saw the officer standing there, with his hand on his gun.

Friendly and unsuspicious by nature, and utterly new to the ways of the Valley, Candida raised the windscreen on her helmet and smiled.

'Hi!' she said cheerfully.

The officer blinked in surprise. He frowned. 'Madam,' he said with polite irritation, 'What are you doing here?'

Candida told him her business, and he stared at her blankly. She could tell that he felt uncertain about whether or not to believe her. At last, probably realizing that he could not very well hold up a whole convoy of officers and jawans while he made up his mind, he swallowed and stepped back. His hand fell away from his gun, but Candida noticed that he kept his eyes fixed cautiously on her hands the whole time. *He must think I'm armed, and will pull a gun on him when he isn't looking,* thought Candida.

'Please come with us,' he requested curtly.

'But ...' stammered Candida, growing alarmed. She glanced at the name badge on his chest. Colonel Sharad Trivedi. She tried again, as calmly as possible. 'I cannot come with you, Colonel. My things are at the Heevan Guest House in Bandipora. I'm headed for Gurais in the morning.'

'We will collect your things from the guest house and then proceed to the army unit,' he said.

She knew, then, that this was not a request. Without another word, she mounted her bike and rode to the town, making straight for the guest house. The thundering wheels of the convoy shook the ground beneath her and filled the air. She took care not to speed up. She didn't wish to arouse suspicion in the men who were following her.

Well, thought Candida, the eternal optimist, *I suppose it could have been worse than getting picked up by the army. I could have got picked up by militants!* And it was while she was laughing at her own silly joke that the idea popped into her head! She just might have a way to convince the colonel that she really was who she had claimed to be ...

Making short work of packing her haversack (she had barely had time to unpack, anyway), she went downstairs to pay for the room. The colonel was waiting for her. *He's probably scared that I'll escape by climbing out of the lobby window!* she thought, amused in spite of her irritation at having her word doubted and her plans ruined this way. There was, apparently, no need to pay for her stay of a few hours. A nod from the colonel, and the bill was considered settled.

'But ...' protested Candida. The owner smiled and shook his head. Resigned, she followed the colonel out to where the convoy was waiting.

'Colonel Trivedi?' she ventured. He turned. 'Is the STD booth on the way to your unit?'

He nodded.

'I'd like to stop there for a moment.'

'For what purpose, ma'am?' he asked. He sounded polite enough, but she did not miss the steely undertone. *Well*, she thought, suddenly raising her chin and her determination all at once. She had a will of her own, and could be equally steely when she chose to be.

'You'll see,' she said coolly, and mounted her bike. Turning to him, she snapped, 'Ready?'

He blinked in momentary surprise. Caught off guard, he nodded and jogged to his truck. Candida rode away at full speed, not bothering with the nicety of waiting for the gargantuan vehicles of the convoy to follow. They did follow, and with haste, apparently fearing that she would get away. Which she did.

'Bloody hell!' exclaimed the colonel, when the first of the trucks turned the bend in the road and there was no leather-clad figure on a bike to be seen. 'Jaldi chalao, Kashi!'

'Ji, saab,' responded the driver, stepping on the accelerator.

They were fairly rattling along at breakneck speed when, suddenly, Kashi threw up his hand and slammed the brakes at the same time. Seeing the precautionary hand, the trucks behind all did likewise.

'What is it?' demanded Colonel Trivedi.

'Woh dekhiye, saab,' said Kashi, pointing to the STD booth. Candida had parked the Royal Enfield and was waiting by the side of the road for them. The colonel jumped down from the truck. From the ones behind, Captain Waghmare and Major Roy did the same well.

Candida led them inside the booth.

'Please check the dialled numbers and the time the call was made,' she said to Colonel Trivedi. Going by how sparsely travelled this road was, she was counting on her call home to be the last dialled number on the list. At a gesture from the colonel, Captain Waghmare stepped up to the instrument and did the needful.

'Koi 0836 STD code wala number hai, sir,' he said.

'If you redial the number, Captain Waghmare,' said Candida, 'my mother will answer. Please ask to speak to me: to Candida Louis. Tell her you are a reporter, looking to interview me for an article you are writing on biking tourism.'

The three officers exchanged glances. Captain Waghmare pressed the redial button. The phone began to ring.

'Hello?' answered Joanna Louis.

'Madam, this is Capta ... I mean Sameer Waghmare this side. May I speak to Candida Louis, please?'

'I'm sorry, Candida is not home,' Candida heard her mother say through the telephone receiver.

'I'm a reporter from the *Times of India*, ma'am. We are doing an article on biking tourism, and I wanted to interview her about it.'

'She is away on a biking tour across India. She will be back only in December.'

'May I call her while she is travelling, ma'am?'

'I'm afraid not. She just called this evening to say that she is in Leh, and her phone is not catching network there.'

'Okay, I'm sorry to have bothered you. Thank you, ma'am.'

He replaced the receiver and nodded to Colonel Trivedi. Slowly, the colonel's face broke into a smile.

'I'm sorry,' he said to Candida, his tone relaxed now. 'But one can't be too careful around these parts.'

Candida grinned and shrugged. 'Told you I wasn't lying, Colonel. I would have googled my name and you could have seen for yourself, but there doesn't seem to be any network in these parts.'

The three officers had undergone a sea change. From stiff, cold military men, they had suddenly transformed into friendly, warm ... *people*!

'There isn't. We manage with our wireless and with the fixed line telephones,' he said.

'I'd like to be heading back to the guest house if that's okay, Colonel,' said Candida.

'No-no, ma'am, you must stay with us at the army camp! We're not far from here and—'

'Is that an order?' she asked, with a twinkle in her eye.

Now, all three officers grinned.

'It's a *request*, ma'am. An invitation.'

'In that case,' said Candida, 'I accept with pleasure!'

They paid for the call and began to leave the booth.

'Mrs Trivedi, I know, will be happy to meet you. Mrs Roy as well, I believe,' said Colonel Trivedi.

Major Roy smiled his assent.

'Have you ever thought of joining the army, ma'am?' asked Captain Waghmare, who had been eyeing Candida with respectful admiration that whole time. 'The forces could do with someone of your courage!'

'Oh no, Captain! That wouldn't suit me at all!' laughed Candida.

'Why not?'

Candida looked at the colonel meaningfully and said, 'I couldn't stand to be bossed around!'

The officers threw back their heads and laughed.

Four days at an army camp left Candida warmer, drier and better fed than she had been since she hit the road in August. She was surrounded by the gallant kindness of the officers (who entreated her at least five times a day to join the army!) and the warmth of their wives. However, Gurais kept calling to her, in a voice that was growing ever-louder. On the fourth night of her stay, she turned to Colonel Trivedi, who, as commanding officer of the unit, was seated at the head of the table. 'Colonel,' she said, 'I would like to leave in the morning.'

'You must stay longer, ma'am! We are enjoying your company so much!'

'I have enjoyed being here too,' she said warmly, looking around the long dinner table to take in all the officers and ladies in a grateful look. 'But I must be on my way, Colonel ...'

And so, with enough sandwiches to last three breakfasts stashed away inside her haversack (courtesy the unit's affectionate, ageing cook), Candida rode out of the army camp at 7 a.m. the next morning. All the officers of the unit turned out to see her off, with the parting injunction that she must call them for help, should she need it.

The road from Bandipora to Gurais was eighty-six kilometres long. Although it called itself a state highway, it was little more than a bumpy dirt road in stretches. The Royal Enfield ascended to the Razdan Pass, a perilous road in the high mountains, that linked Gurais with the rest of the world. It was so

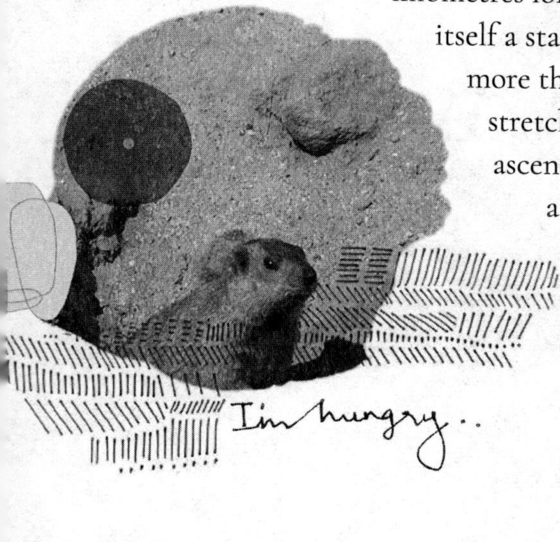

narrow in places that a vehicle had to steer a perfect course in order not to get pitched over the edge. Unsecured by guardrails, the drop was a free fall of a few thousand feet. The Royal Enfield, however, remained true to course, and descended into the Gurais valley a few hours later.

There she stood. Habba Khatoon. Lofty and majestic, breathtakingly beautiful as the poetess for whom she had been named, the woman who had once trod the very earth upon which Candida now stood, looking for her lost love. Queen among the peaks that surrounded the valley of Gurais, Habba Khatoon was unmistakable. She stood out. She stood alone.

Candida felt tears start in her eyes as she lingered beside the gushing Kishanganga in Dawar village. Unable to tear her gaze away from the pyramid-shaped summit ahead of her, she knew not if her tears were of sadness or of joy. Or whether, inexplicably, they had sprung from a sense of coming home ...

MAID OF SNOW
fearless
Kashgar
Jammu and Kashmir Area
I am strong & shy
CHINA
PAKISTAN
Jammu
and
Gilgit
LOC
K A R A K O R A M
H I M A L A Y A
DEOSAI MOUNTAINS
LINE OF CONTROL
SALTORO RANGE
LADAKH
Mintaka Pass
Khunjerab Pass
Batura Muztagh
Baltit
Hispar Muztagh
Hispar Glacier
Rakaposhi Range
Chogo Lungma Glacier
Haramosh Range
Biafo Glacier
Baltoro Muztagh
Baltoro Glacier
Mt Godwin Austen (K2)
Masherbrum Range
Siachen Glacier
Siachen Muztagh
Karakoram Pass
Chilas
Astor
Skardu
Nanga Parbat
Babusar Pass
Kel
Muzaffarabad
Tithwal
Wular Lake
Zoji La
Dras
Kargil
Indus
Nubra
Shyok
Yarkand
Goma
NJ980420
Sia La
Bilafond La
75°
76°
77°
78°
37°
36°
35°

MAID OF SNOW

Kashmir – Part 2

The tourist bungalow in Dawar, the headquarters of Gurais Valley, was a long, low building of grey stone, with a pink tiled roof and an uninterrupted view of the Habba Khatoon peak from its front door. It was basic but comfortable, and only served breakfast. However, just beside it was Noorani, a quaint little restaurant that everybody who ever passed that way, visited. Her tummy was rumbling now, so Candida put away her camera and descended the slope to Noorani, where she wolfed down a delicious meal of omelettes, mutton and the local unleavened bread called lawaas. She thought, with fleeting regret, of the remaining sandwiches in her haversack, and knew that she should not waste them.

I won't! she argued with herself as she washed the lawaas down with chai. *I'll eat them later. In the morning. For breakfast. Promise!*

Fine. I believe you, smirked the other voice in her head.

Over the next three days, she rode into the surrounding villages of Gurais and the neighbouring Tulail Valley. At 8000 feet above sea level, one could only travel there when the weather permitted, which was five months in the year. For the rest of the time, Gurais and its neighbouring villages would be buried under twenty feet of snow, lost to the world.

The people she met were wary at first. Their homes were within sight of the Line of Control that separated the Indian from Pakistan administered Kashmir. Militancy, firing and unrest were not unfamiliar to them. However, Candida found that if she kept her manner unobtrusive and friendly, they responded warmly enough. The Dards, the tribe that populated this region, were by nature hospitable. But Candida was amused to find that, without exception, every time she arrived at a village, the people reacted with astonishment! A young woman in trousers riding on a bike ... a *motor*bike*!* Alone ... *ALONE??* ... in Gurais! Unbelievable! In every village she entered, the locals surrounded her instantly, the young men to gawk at the Royal Enfield, the elderly to gawk at Candida, and the children to yell joyfully, cut capers around the two and shake hands. In Chakwali, one little boy actually turned six somersaults in rapid succession to express his glee at the sight of the motorbike. Unable to resist, Candida bent down and hugged him. He was a beautiful child, pink-cheeked, with hazel brown eyes and golden hair. But the instant she did that, little Hasan stiffened. His smile vanished and he hung his head, glancing furtively at his friends, who had, likewise, all fallen silent. Candida let her arms drop to her sides. She knew she had made a mistake. She had embarrassed Hasan in front of his mates. But she smiled down at the children, noticing that they were all as lovely as Hasan. Diving into her haversack, she came up with a handful of toffees that she distributed among them. They immediately brightened and decided to go back to being on friendly terms with this lady after all! Presently, they stood around sucking on the sweets with animated enjoyment.

An old man was sitting on some steps nearby, watching. Candida looked up and caught his eyes on her. She raised her palm to her forehead in salaam, and he returned the greeting. She went across to sit down beside him, while the children crawled all over the Royal Enfield, making themselves at home on it. With one eye on them and the other on her companion, she introduced herself. To her joy, she found that he spoke Urdu, which she could understand.

'I am Jamal Mir. I am a hundred years old,' he said, matter-of-factly.

Candida was startled. He did look ancient, it was true, but a *hundred*? 'When were you born, Chacha?' she asked.

'When the snow was falling outside and our homes were buried under it, my mother told me.'

She smiled at this simple description of a birthday. Momentarily, her mind flashed back to the birthday parties that Mamma had thrown for her when she was a child. But Jamal Mir was speaking again and she turned her attention back to him. He looked like he had a story to tell, and she did not want to miss a word of it.

'... would come and go all the time. It was a busy place, full of bustle and importance because everybody had to pass through Chakwali if they wanted to go across to Gilgit and Kashgar.' He smiled proudly and added, 'They would carry potatoes with them.'

Candida frowned, not understanding his meaning. Potatoes ... to eat on the journey?

'They would bring back apples in exchange,' he added.

Oh, trade! thought Candida, catching on. True. Gurais had been the gateway to Central Asia on the ancient Silk Route. Candida remembered studying about it in 7th grade. Jamal Mir had probably never heard the term 'Silk Route'. He was merely describing the experience of living on it.

A tall, middle-aged fellow approached and greeted the old man. 'Tey je khal heng?' he enquired in Shina, the language of the Dardic people.

'I am well,' replied Jamal Mir, nodding. The man walked on and Jamal continued with his story.

'They came in caravans or on horses. A few even came on foot. They always stopped here to rest. They stayed with us. Sometimes strangers, sometimes friends.'

'The traders were your friends?'

'They become our friends in time,' he replied, 'after three or four trips. They told us stories from over there ...' and he pointed towards the mountains in the northwest.

'They told us stories about the people they exchanged things with. About their homes, their children ...' His voice trailed off, his eyes gazing into a past that she could not follow him into. 'Friends ...' he murmured softly to himself, sadly.

The children were sitting on the bike seat now, pretending to rev the engine. They made loud sounds to imitate the roar of a speeding bike, and then fell about laughing at their own genius! After watching them in amusement, Candida turned her attention back to the old man, for he had resumed speaking.

'After 1947, people stopped coming here. No more potatoes and apples. No more friends. Everybody has forgotten us, now.'

As Candida looked about her, she realized that Gurais was, indeed, a lonely place. Perhaps one of the loneliest places in the world. Maybe that was why the hearts of its people were still simple, their traditions untouched, their culture untainted by outside influences. Each village was like an isolated island. They cultivated potatoes along the fertile banks of the Kishanganga, and tended to their livestock. As she watched, a group of women came down the slope carrying baskets on their backs, piled high with logs of wood that they had been cutting and gathering. Candida stared, open-mouthed, at how effortlessly they bore their burden.

One young woman walking past murmured, 'Salaam-aleykum.'

'Waleykum asalaam, Aa'idah. Mas whai piyo rakhtamus,' Jamal Mir said to her in Shina. She nodded her assent. Then, remembering his guest, he called out hurriedly, 'Du!' She gave a half-smile and kept walking.

'My great-grandson's wife,' he said to Candida, switching back to Urdu again. 'I have asked her for two glasses of water for us.' Candida watched Aa'idah offload the basket of logs onto the wood pile outside their home. *The logs must weigh at least forty kilos*, mused Candida, truly impressed by the strength in the woman's deceptively frail body. Seeing the direction of her gaze, the old man explained, 'Five months in the year we are buried under snow. Twenty, sometimes thirty feet high the snow comes. We must stay inside our homes and sit around the bukhari to keep warm. In the summer months, our women collect wood for the bukhari and stock up in preparation for the following winter.'

'How much wood is needed?'

'About fifty or sixty kilos a day.'

Candida's jaw dropped open. Aa'idah came out bearing two glasses of water. She smiled gently at her guest and gestured invitingly towards the house. The old man led the way inside, where the womenfolk of his family were brewing nuun chai. Candida joined them on the floor, sitting cross-legged and looking around her. The house was made entirely of wooden logs piled one on top of the other with not a nut or a bolt to hold them in place. In fact, every house in Chakwali and the surrounding villages was fashioned in the same way.

'It keeps the snow out and the heat in,' explained Jamal Mir, sipping his tea. 'It can withstand even the earthquakes that happen here from time to time,' he chuckled. He gestured for Candida to begin, and she raised her cup to her lips. The tea was pink and salty! The women handed around buttered lawaas, which was to be dipped in the brew and consumed. The combination was delicious, and the piping hot tea warmed her immediately.

Presently, a large, friendly goat poked its head around the front door. The children were eating something out of a plastic bag, and the rustling sound had brought the animal there to inquire into the matter. When he had confirmed his guess that there was a treat to be had in the vicinity, he invited himself inside to claim his share, butting the bag and jumping on the children when they pushed him away. The women laughed, and one got up and shooed the goat outside. The animal left in high dudgeon. Candida got the distinct feeling it would avenge this insult, and soon!

When tea was finished, Candida thanked the women and stepped outside the log house, while Jamal stayed behind to discuss the weaving that his womenfolk were to begin. The front door was built high above the ground, probably to hold out against snow piling up and blocking it too early in the winter. A roughly-hewn wooden ramp served to convey people from the house down to the street below. Halfway along the ramp, Candida stopped and looked out towards the west, where Pakistan lay. Chakwali was, in fact, the last village on the Indian side of the Line of Control. Civilians were not allowed beyond this point.

'At night, we often hear artillery firing,' said Jamal quietly. He had come to stand behind her while she had been lost in reverie. 'I wonder if my brother is still alive over there.' He jerked his head towards the west.

'Your brother lives in Pakistan?'

'In 1947, he went as usual to trade with the people there, while my parents and sisters and I remained behind at home. Suddenly, a line was drawn. This side became India, that side Pakistan. We could no longer freely travel from one side to the other like we used to. We never saw my brother again. Anyway, it is better if he is dead. What is the use of living for so long? No use. I should know!' and the old man laughed heartily at himself. Candida watched his merriment with a sense of wonder. These people had so little that they sometimes had to melt snow to drink in the absence of water during the winter months. There was no television, no amenities, no links to the outside world, or even to the rest of the country to which they were supposed to belong. The nearest school was fourteen kilometres away, and the children had to trudge there on foot. Snowfall, shelling and infiltration ensured that their attendance was sporadic at best. And yet, this man, who had seen this life for a hundred years or close to it, could still find a reason to laugh.

As she bid goodbye to her friend, Candida took out as much money as she could spare and pressed it into his hands. He started to protest vociferously, but then he saw that she was crying. Averting his eyes quickly, he said no more.

As Candida rode away from Chakwali, she stopped and turned to get a last glimpse of what she was leaving behind. People were bustling about their work. A herd of goats scrambled up a slope, shepherded on by a man with a stick. Snow-covered peaks stood like sentinels in the background, grimly watching over a people that the rest of the world had forgotten. She saw a valley, green and lush, and a river running through it. She turned around and rode away then. Perhaps she might never return to this place. But at twenty-four, never is too long a time to know.

The girls, old and young, big and small, sat around the bukhari listening intently to the lesson. All was quiet outside, and inside the classroom Asma Miss taught on about World War II, a man named Hitler and the Yahudis. The story was interesting; there was pin drop silence in the class. Then, from the distance came a rumbling sound. Nobody noticed it at first. But as it gradually grew into a roar, the girls closest to the window raised their heads to look outside for the source of the noise. Up the winding mountain road appeared a figure on a motorbike. A man wearing a heavy jacket, jeans, thick black boots and a helmet. He even wore gloves on his hands. A militant! This might be a militant!

Their hearts stood still in terror. Asma Miss stopped teaching, and hurried to join the little group huddled together at the window. Fear coursed through her body and rose up to grip her throat. *No!* she thought, giving herself a mental shake. *I must pull myself together for the sake of the girls.*

At that moment, the motorbike pulled up in front of the tiny school building. The man lowered his booted feet to the ground. Slowly, he raised his hand, lifted the helmet off his head ... and a cascade of thick long hair came tumbling down his shoulders!

A woman! A female, just like them, only riding a bike! A thrill of excitement shot through the watching girls, galvanizing them into action. They ran outside, pell-mell, to come up panting before the Royal Enfield. Candida looked at them in surprise. She could not know what they were thinking. Being a girl from a safe, sleepy town like Hubballi in the south of India, and now residing in the bustling metropolis of Bangalore, she could not possibly guess at the impact her arrival had on a group of girls in a small Kashmiri village like this one. So, she didn't know that behind the hijab that covered their heads and almost all of their faces, they were grinning happily at her. Asma Miss came hurrying out behind the girls and greeted Candida with a salaam.

'My girls are so happy to see woman riding bike, madam,' she said. 'They have never seen before. To tell you truth, I also have not seen.' She spoke in English, slowly and succinctly. The smile in her voice and eyes was unmistakable. 'May I ask where you are coming from?'

'From Bangalore in Karnataka,' replied Candida. Her listeners immediately grew animated.

'Girls!' cried Asma Miss, 'you know where it is, na? I taught in Geography class, you remember?'

Immediately one little girl squatted down in the dirt, and drew the outline of India with her finger. Then, she pointed proudly to where Karnataka would be.

'Very good, Noora!' applauded her teacher. 'It is correct, what you have shown! Well done!'

Meanwhile, the others had sidled up to Candida, as if unable to stay away any longer. One child reached out tentatively and touched the bike before withdrawing her hand shyly, as if surprised at her own daring. Gently, Candida reached out and took the little hand. She brought it forward and placed it on the bike. The child's eyes widened. Gaining courage, she stroked the petrol tank and handles, wonderingly.

'Didi, what you are doing in Gurais?' asked one of the older girls in the group.

'I'm riding across India on a motorcycle,' replied Candida, touched by the guileless enthusiasm of the group around her. They gasped at her answer. '*Alone* travelling on motorcycle?'

Candida nodded.

'Everywhere? Full India?'

She nodded again, and this time was unable to suppress a smile.

'Didi!' exclaimed the girls, 'We want to grow up and become like you!'

'You want to grow up and ride on a motorbike?' asked Candida. They nodded, their eyes bursting with smiles as their teacher stood back and silently enjoyed their happiness.

'But you don't have to wait to grow up. You can do that right now,' said Candida.

'Now?'

'Now!' cried Candida, swinging the smallest little girl off her feet and seating her on the petrol tank in front of her. Before the child or her classmates could recover from their surprise, Candida zoomed away, enjoying the squeals of delight from her young charge, and from those they had left behind. She took her on a short spin up and down the road, and then returned to the waiting group.

'Me! Me!' cried the others, clamouring for a turn on the Royal Enfield.

'Nahin, nahin, bachche, please don't trouble Didi,' said Asma Miss, hurrying forward to break up the confusion.

'But, I'm enjoying it!' grinned Candida. And for the next half hour she ferried girls of all shapes and sizes on her bike, enjoying their delight as much as they enjoyed the experience! On each ride, she put a smaller child in front of her on the petrol tank (where she herself had once sat with Daddy and imagined she was flying!), and a taller one behind her.

'Now hold on tight!' she would cry, feeling the arms come around her waist, hearing their giggles and squeals of joy as she rode away. She went through this motion until each of them had had a turn. When the last one slid off the Royal Enfield, Candida turned to the teacher. Asma's reluctance to cause inconvenience could not withstand the kind smile and the inviting hand extended to her. With a laugh, Asma climbed on behind Candida and they were off to the tumultuous sounds of clapping and cheering from the watching students.

Before she left, Candida pulled out her cell phone. There wasn't a scrap of network to be caught, but its camera worked fine, and she intended to put it to good use. She clicked lots of pictures of the girls around the bike, and herself with them. This meeting was one she wanted to remember forever, and narrate to her great grandchildren someday, perhaps when she was as old as Jamal Mir!

Back in Dawar, Candida ate dinner at Noorani and turned in early. She intended to leave Gurais at first

light and ride straight on through to Srinagar. It would be difficult to leave these mountains and this river, the innocence and harshness, the paucity and abundance, the joy and the sorrow that dwelt here side-by-side. If she broke journey at Bandipora, she didn't trust herself not to turn the Royal Enfield and come straight back to Gurais.

Early the next morning, Candida stepped out of the tourist bungalow and stood gazing at the Habba Khatoon. The first ray of the sun had fallen upon it like a benediction, and Candida shut her eyes, capturing the sight in all its glory behind her closed eyelids. Then she mounted the Royal Enfield and rode away.

There would be times in Bangalore, as she sat behind her desk at work computing numbers, when she would remember that somewhere in the world stood a range of mountains. And then her spirit would rise up and rush away to re-join them, to dance in their laps and wander in their midst, free. Candida Louis had left her fish in the Unkal Lake, and her tears in Chandra Tal.

Her heart, she left behind her in Gurais ...

OF GHOSTS AND OTHER THINGS

OF GHOSTS AND OTHER THINGS

Rajasthan

She was there to buy an LED headlight for the night rides. They were there to rent bikes.

'You travelling alone?' asked Oliver, strolling up to where Candida was carrying out the operation of fitting the LED to the front of the Royal Enfield.

'Yup,' she said, not looking up from her work.

'Need a hand?'

'No, I'm good. I've done this before.'

'So I see. I'm Oliver, by the way. From—'

'Australia. Yes, I gathered from your accent,' she said, standing up and dusting her hands. She grinned at him. 'Finished!' she declared, then checked her handiwork by turning on the bike. The light flashed on, stark and bright.

'Well done!' he nodded. 'How do you know so much about bikes?'

'I don't know about anything *except* bikes. They're all I know, really. My Dad tells me I was born on a bike.'

'You don't say! Seriously?'

'Nah,' she said. 'But I've been on one ever since I could sit up. We're all bike-crazy in my family, and my best friend's father owns a garage, where I used to go after college and help out.'

Oliver turned around and called, 'Will! Hey, William! Grab Jack and Eddie and come on over here and meet this young lady!'

Three more tall, strapping Australians wandered up and were introduced. They looked like they were in their fifties, and appeared friendly, except for Ed, who only nodded, poker-faced, to Candida and went back to filling out the rental forms.

'So what are you doing so far from home?' asked Candida.

'Just travelling, seeing places. You?'

'I'm riding through India on a motorcycle.'

All three did a double take, and even Ed raised his head from the forms to stare at her.

'*Alone*?' asked Oliver.

'Mm-hmm.'

'That's ... pretty cool,' said Oliver, clearly impressed. 'How old are you, twenty-five?'

'Twenty-four, actually,' she corrected.

Suddenly the guy called Jack burst out laughing. The others stared at him blankly till he stopped and shook his head at Candida. 'I'm sorry, I wasn't laughing at you.'

'Who, then?' she enquired.

'At the four of *us*, actually!' said Jack.

'Oi!' protested William. 'I liked it better when I thought you were laughing at *her*!'

'Jack,' said Oliver sternly, 'explain yourself.'

'Well, it's just that the four of us promised each other way back in college that we'd get great jobs, find great wives, earn loads of money, and then travel the world. But now I see ...' indicating Candida, 'that we wasted thirty years doing all that boring stuff! We began at the wrong end, whereas this kid here got it right!'

Candida laughed, while the others looked crestfallen.

'Never mind,' she said, 'it's never too late!'

'Where you headed to from Bikaner?' asked Oliver.

'I only just got in from Amritsar. I'm going to Jaisalmer from here, then Pali, and then on to Jodhpur. I have some important stuff to do at Jaisalmer,' she replied with a twinkle in her eye.

'What?' asked William eagerly.

'There's a haunted village near Jaisalmer I'd like to—'

'Coffee!' grunted Ed, landing in their midst without the slightest idea of having barged in on an interesting conversation.

'Will you join us?' asked Oliver, turning to Candida.

'If I won't be in the way.'

'Not at all! We'd like to hear more about this haunted village. Just because our need for coffee momentarily waylaid us, doesn't mean we are not intrigued!'

Seated around a table at a Café Coffee Day outlet, with their hands wrapped about mugs of foaming cappuccinos, Candida told them all about her stay in Amritsar and her visit to the sacred Sikh shrine called the Golden Temple. She reminisced about the tall, thick, delicious glasses of lassi that kindly villagers had offered her in earthen pots as she rode through field after golden field of mustard, so typical of rural Punjab. Then there was her visit to the India-Pakistan international border. On the Indian side was the village of Attari, on Pakistan's was Wagah. Both armies manned the gates of their respective countries, leaving a few feet of space in between as the no man's land. The gates were opened in the day and then closed in an elaborate military ceremony each evening!

The Aussies listened to Candida in fascination. Finally Oliver said, 'You were about to tell us something about a village near Jaisalmer?'

'A *haunted* village near Jaisalmer,' she corrected with a laugh. 'It is called Kuldhara. The story goes like this: Kuldhara, not far from Sam, was an old abandoned ruin, a ghost town. A community of Paliwal Brahmins had lived there for many centuries quite happily and prosperously. But, sometime in the 1800s, the king's minister, who was a corrupt and debauched fellow, came upon the Paliwal chieftain's lovely young daughter. He threatened to double the taxes of Kuldhara if its people did not hand her to him in marriage. When he arrived the next day to claim his bride, he found an abandoned town, with not a soul in it. The Paliwals had vacated the village in the dead of night, leaving behind them a curse that it would never again be occupied. Nobody ever learnt of their whereabouts, or encountered them again. It is said that the village is now occupied by none but the spirits of the Paliwal Brahmins.'

The Australians promptly asked if they could join her on her travels through Rajasthan.

'Sure, as long as you guys don't mind roughing it. I'm on a pretty tight budget.'

'No problem!' they said in unison and drained their coffee mugs.

Two hours later, they had found an inexpensive hotel that was clean but basic, with none of the trappings of television, Wi-Fi and a swimming pool. This didn't bother them in the least because they intended to make full use of their one day in Bikaner to explore the place, before leaving for Jaisalmer. The four men shared two rooms between them, and Candida got a tiny single to herself.

They put down their bags and set off to look around the place on foot.

'Movie theatre!' exclaimed Ed suddenly, and before Candida could react, the four Australians had taken off at a run to get a closer look (ogle?) at the posters mounted on the boards outside an old, single-entry theatre across the street. Candida joined them at a more leisurely place. Their mouths were agape and they looked positively enthralled!

'Boy, you guys are easy to please!' chuckled Candida. 'What will you do when you see the sunset over the sand dunes? Don't you want to save some excitement for that stuff, too?' They didn't seem to hear her.

The posters on display announced the latest film releases ... that all turned out to be several months old! On closer examination, Candida observed that there were hardly any people about. Only one man—probably a caretaker—was pottering about the place, which had none of the bustle of an active cinema hall. This theatre seemed to be defunct.

'Let's go watch a movie!' suggested Oliver.

The others agreed heartily.

'But—' began Candida.

'No buts. Come on, we're crazy about Indian movies. They're the best!'

'Watch them on YouTube then,' said Candida unfeelingly.

'Not the same thing,' said William. 'Seeing it on the big screen ... oh boy!'

She watched them in amusement. They were her dad's age, but were behaving like kids in a candy shop! They stood around looking at her so imploringly that she decided to put them out of their misery as quickly as possible.

'The theatre is defunct, you know?'

However, at this piece of news, they looked so dismayed that she added quickly, 'But let me see what I can do.' She hurried across to the box office where the caretaker was cleaning up. 'Bhaiyyaji,' she hailed him politely, 'we want to watch a movie.'

The man looked at her for a long moment, as if trying to gauge her mental balance. Then he shook his head and replied, 'Sorry madam, theatre bandh hai.'

'I know it is shut, bhaiyyaji,' she continued, 'But those people there ...' she pointed to the four hopeful humans standing nearby, 'are foreigners, and are desperate to watch a Hindi movie. Mehmaan hain woh Rajasthan ke, bhaiyyaji. They are guests of Rajasthan! How can we refuse them?'

She knew that in Rajasthan a guest was considered god, and therefore could not be denied anything. It was a smart move. The man immediately relented.

'I don't have any feature films, madamji. But I have lots of old Hindi film trailers and songs. Will that do?'

'Nicely!' she said gratefully. And the next thing they knew, all five of them were seated in the very first row of the sprawling cinema hall, directly below the screen, staring up at it.

'Why don't we move a little more to the back?' asked Jack, turning around and eyeing the rows upon rows of empty seats behind them.

'This way you get the full impact,' said Candida. If she had to watch Hindi film trailers during her one evening in Bikaner instead of exploring the city as she had hoped to, she might as well extract some revenge for it. If this was their idea of fun, then hers was to give them all a good crick in the neck!

Candida never expected to enjoy the evening so much, but she actually ended up doing just that. For, halfway through the first song, William and Jack jumped up and began to dance. Australian gyrations to 'Didi tera devar deevana' were irresistibly funny! And two more earnest performers than Will and Jack one might never hope to encounter, not even in Bollywood!

The next morning, setting out early by mutual agreement, the five travellers explored whatever they could of Bikaner in half a day. They would need to leave for Jaisalmer (six hours away) by afternoon if they were to visit Gajaner Lake en route and still reach Jaisalmer before nightfall.

Built in the late 1500s, Bikaner's Junagarh fort was beautiful and well-preserved. (Candida was to encounter a very different circumstance at Jaisalmer, but we'll get to that when she does.) It was one of the few forts in Rajasthan that was not situated atop a hill. Made of red sandstone and marble of different varieties, the fort complex consisted of a number of rooms and palaces, each uniquely designed and decorated. While Maharaja Rao Jodha had ruled over Jodhpur, his second son, Rao Bika, realized that his chances of ascending his father's throne were bleak. So he conquered a large territory northwest of Jodhpur and made it his capital.

'Hence the name Bikaner,' explained the tour guide they had hired at the entrance. 'You know, in spite of many attempts, the Mughals did not manage to occupy this fort except on one occasion,' he added proudly.

'How long did that occupation last?' asked William.

'One day!' declared the guide, and walked away to the next room.

The road to Jaisalmer was good, but passed through desert vistas that provided little variety for the eye. The chief impression left in Candida's mind was 'sandy', for what with the Thar running along one side, the five of them were soon covered in layers of sand!

They entered Jaisalmer at 9 p.m., when everything was dark and only the fort stood lit up. Made of yellow sandstone, it shone golden in the glow of the powerful footlights trained upon it, giving the visitor a sense of awe at its ethereal beauty. The walls were high and rugged, and dotted with watch towers from which one could imagine Raja Jaisal's sentinels observing everything, yet revealing nothing of the treasure-trove of fine architecture concealed behind it.

'Tomorrow ...' Candida promised herself, feeling her heart clench with eager anticipation at the thought of exploring this fortress. They rode straight to the small guest house that Oliver had found over the internet, and that Google Maps led them directly to.

Jaisalmer had little natural colour. Everything, as far as the eye could see, was tawny as a lion's mane – houses, fort and the sandy earth upon which they stood. Nearly treeless in its aspect, all its hues came from the splendid clothes of its people – the brilliant turbans of the menfolk, the colourful saris and lehenga cholis of the women. After an enjoyable breakfast of bajre ki roti and lehsun chutney at a wayside restaurant the following morning, the five friends made their way to the Jaisalmer fort.

'Perfect,' muttered Candida, as she stood at the entrance looking up at it.

'What is?' enquired Jack.

'The way this place is camouflaged. They've built it from the local material so that it doesn't stand out from its desert environment. From a distance, one could almost mistake it for being a craggy hill. Must have effectively kept the enemies away.'

'Were they at war a lot?' asked Ed.

'The Rajputs? Constantly! With each other, with the Mughals, with invaders from Central Asia. War was their main business, I imagine. Let's go inside.'

To their great surprise, they found themselves inside a 'living' fort. Nothing here was a monument on display, a relic from past glories. It was very much present, living and breathing with families and traders whose home it was. People were cooking and cleaning; cattle meandered through the alleyways, casually tearing off posters from the walls and chewing on them; children tumbled around on doorsteps or swung off the branches of low trees. Somewhere, a film shooting was in progress. The discovery of this launched Ed into seventh heaven! He ran straight towards the sets and disappeared into the milieu of lights and cameras before the others could stop him. Seeing Candida's exasperation, William, trying to look nonchalant, cleared his throat and said, 'Er, I'll just go and get him, then. Be back in a moment,' and he too disappeared after Ed.

The other two stood around looking at their toes, all the while casting furtive glances, filled quite clearly with longing towards where their mates had vanished. Candida watched them with a mix of amusement and irritation. Finally, taking pity on them she sighed, 'Fine, go!'

They darted away instantly like bats out of hell, and she called after them, 'I'm going exploring. Call me when you guys are done!'

She wandered off by herself and visited some of the Jain temples with their intricate architecture and superbly depicted stone carvings. The jewel among them—the Parshwanath temple—was particularly stunning. After visiting three out of the seven temples, Candida decided to then wander at leisure and stop to examine anything that grabbed her fancy. She could have hired a tour guide to show her around, but she had never been one for factual details and book learning. She preferred the satisfaction of discovering for herself the little secrets that places like this tended to harbour.

It was not for no reason that this 12th century fort was named Sonar Qila. It was truly 'golden', because the locally available yellow sandstone had been employed in the construction of just about everything here. There were the most attractive fabrics and trinkets on display, and the place was a regular shopper's paradise, if one was into that sort of thing. Candida was not, but the lure of the splendid tapestry, dancing mirror work and gorgeous embroidery all around proved irresistible. Without knowing how, she found herself inside one of the shops. When she walked out of there a half-hour later, she had bought a bedspread for her parents and a lovely mirror work bag for herself. Only the fact that she was broke propelled her to the entrance of the store and forced her to keep walking without looking back!

Now Candida began to notice the lateness of the hour. It was almost 3 o'clock! No wonder her stomach was rumbling. She had forgotten to have lunch. Where were the guys? There was no missed call from them. Odd. She made her way back to the film set and walked inside, looking for her friends. There were some junior artists dressed as British army officers, and others dressed as royal servants, courtiers and guards. This was clearly a period film. On the other side, the dance director and his troupe were lounging about drinking tea. The set assistants and production people were scurrying around getting things organized. But where were the Australians? Had they left and perhaps forgotten to call ...?

'Candida! Oi, Candi! Over here!' came Ollie's voice. She spun around in every direction but couldn't spot them anywhere. Suddenly, she saw the junior artists dressed in British army uniforms approaching her. She gave one keen look and her eyes nearly popped out of her head!

'What the hell are you doing?' she squeaked incredulously. But the four Australians only smiled broadly, looking shy and proud and a little foolish all at the same time.

'Are you …? Did they …? I mean, did you get *hired* in the film??'

'Told'ja she wouldn't believe it, hey?' chuckled Ollie.

'Guess you were right about that, mate,' shrugged William.

'The director took one look at us and offered us the part right away!' beamed Jack.

'And you *accepted*?' demanded Candida.

'Well, Ed here did. We just went along to keep him out of trouble!'

Candida swallowed. She gulped. A strange sound escaped her. She frankly turned and ran from the sets, leaving the others to stare after her blankly. Outside, she leaned against a wall and laughed till the tears poured down her cheeks. They were the funniest sight, complete oddballs, and completely lovable, those four silly friends of hers! Shaking her head and wiping her eyes, she rearranged her face into decorous lines and went back inside to rejoin them. She found them looking anxiously for her, wondering if she had suddenly taken ill.

'No, nothing,' she answered to their inquiries, and quickly changed the subject. 'You guys coming back to the hotel anytime soon?'

'The director says it will be another two hours. Are you tired?' asked Ollie, concerned.

'No, I'll get a bite to eat and then explore some more. Except, oh!'

'What?' they asked in unison.

'You guys didn't get to see the Jaisalmer fort at all! And we leave tomorrow evening for Sam.'

'Hey,' said Jack with a grin, 'We're movie stars! Nothing else matters!'

The sand dunes of Sam were forty-two kilometres outside Jaisalmer city. They were ... otherworldly. Not far into the desert was the India-Pakistan border, which added a sense of dangerous charm to the place for Candida. To the Australians, of course, it meant nothing.

They had rented tents for the night, pitched right there in the sands. Dropping their things off, they went out on camel back to witness the sunset over the dunes.

As she sat in the wind-combed sands watching the gigantic orange orb sink over the horizon, Candida thought, *After it sets here, this same sun will set a little later over the lands of Pakistan. Are we all so different from each other, then? If people remembered to watch sunsets, they would find it difficult to fight wars.* Unbidden came the memory of Jamal Mir and his brother, turned into enemies one sudden day by a pencil line hastily scratched across a map ...

Then, a young Rajasthani boy, a woman, and an older man appeared over the western edge of the dune. For a moment, they stood silhouetted against the setting sun, little knowing what a beautiful picture they made. Dressed in the traditional garb of the desert people, they approached and bowed with folded hands.

'May we perform for you?' they asked in a mix of Hindi and Rajasthani. Candida nodded, seeing that her companions were as eager as herself for the performance. The father carried with him the Ravanahatha, an instrument made of a small gourd with strings running up along its arm. The man drew his bow and began to play a haunting tune. Every beat was highlighted by the jerk of his arm, which sent the bells on the end of the bow jingling. The boy sang in a high-pitched, flawless voice, while the woman danced. The experience was enthralling. The woman was superbly supple, twirling and swinging with consummate skill. Dark of skin, large eyes outlined thickly with kohl, mouth coated with lipstick that almost, *almost* hid the greenish stubble growing over her upper lip.

Candida gasped in surprise and quickly turned it into a cough. When the performers received praise and money from each member of their audience, they disappeared over the dune from where they had come.

'How well she dances!' exclaimed William.

'You liked her?' asked Candida.

'She was lovely!' he sighed dreamily.

'Good. Because *she*,' said Candida wryly, 'was a *he*!'

The next day, after a breakfast of methi bajra puri and aloo ki subzi, the five rode to the ghost village. Kuldhara ...

The five friends wandered over the ruins curiously. The place carried an air of haunting sadness, and even natural vegetation seemed reluctant to grow there. How could a place in the wilderness be so devoid of life?

'If we came here at night, would we encounter a ghost?' mused Candida.

'Probably many ghosts,' said William with a quiet shiver.

But they were never to find out, because the people of the neighbouring villages came across and locked the gates of Kuldhara unfailingly every night. If, indeed, there was a curse laid upon it by its former inhabitants, Kuldhara had been held in its grip these past two hundred years. For, not even the creatures of the wild had seen fit to make their home there.

After a trek to the Parashuraama Mahadev Temple nestled in a cave at the foot of the Aravalli hills outside Pali, it was time to head for Jodhpur. The climb had been challenging, and the view it afforded of the Mewar region had been worth the effort. Ed had been particularly taken with the langurs along the way, with whom he generously shared the prasad he had received at the temple.

'Terrific, Ed!' exclaimed Ollie. 'You can finally go back and tell Marla that you made some friends in India!'

The others laughed as they mounted their bikes. Then Jack, who had been looking a little puzzled for a while asked, 'Has anybody seen my bike keys?'

'No, mate. Lose it, did you?' replied William. Everyone dismounted and went to help Jack look. It was not in the ignition or anywhere around the bike.

'Does your pocket have a hole, by any chance?' asked Candida, worriedly. Jack checked. Nope, none. They retraced their steps to the temple area, peering closely at the ground as they went. A few pilgrims, seeing their distress, joined in the search. The group slowly returned to the bikes, all the while scanning the ground. Suddenly, one pilgrim looked up and pointed excitedly to Jack's bike.

'Woh rahin chabiyaan!' she cried. Sure enough, the bike keys were lying on the seat of Jack's Bullet! The five friends stared in surprise. The keys had definitely not been there earlier. Where had they appeared from? The lady dropped to her knees and began to pray and exult, 'It's a miracle! Om Banna ki jai!'

Candida raised her eyebrows in surprise. Om Banna?

'You must stop at Om Banna and thank him for his help! The temple is not far from here. On your way to Jodhpur only it is. Go on, jaldi!' cried the pilgrims. Before the five could seek an explanation, they found themselves mounting their bikes and riding away!

A little ahead, they pulled up to the side of the road. Taking out her phone, Candida googled 'Om Banna'. As she read about it, her face broke into a broad grin. 'Sounds like our kind of place, guys. The deity of this temple is a motorbike!'

The story of Om Banna went like this: On a cold winter's day in 1991, a man called Om Singh Rathore (aka Om Banna) had been riding his Royal Enfield Bullet somewhere in that very area, when he crashed into a tree and died. The police took away the bike to hold as evidence. The next morning, the bike went missing from the police chowki, and was found in the same place where its beloved master had died. The police retrieved it, emptied the petrol tank and kept it under lock and key. The next day, the bike was gone again, and was once again found at the accident site. Believing this to be engineered by the spirit of Om Banna, the locals erected a glass case around the bike and began to worship it. Now it was believed that Om Banna wandered the area as a benevolent ghost, helping travellers in distress.

'By returning their lost keys!' cried William, and everyone laughed. They were at the temple now, and this irreverent behaviour attracted angry glares from the locals around. Rearranging their faces into expressions of piety, they quickly bowed before the glass-enclosed Royal Enfield Bullet bearing the registration number RNJ 7773. William mumbled, 'Thank you, Om Banna, for finding this dolt Jack's bike keys. Thanks for a great trip to Rajasthan. And, if you had a hand in it, thanks for sending us Candida. Our journey wouldn't have been this terrific without her!'

'Hear, hear!' mumbled Oliver, Ed and William under their breaths.

Hands folded, eyes closed and head bent, Candida smiled quietly to herself.

A TRUNK FULL OF WATER

A sea with no beach.
A city with no boundaries.
There was Varkala, and there was the sea,
and nothing else between them.

Varkala: Siraj's Homestay
THE HAVEN...
It's costing me stories
to stay here...
isn't that really
cool & amazing?

Spik

This is
most b
places I

Printed by Guru Digital Printers, Shivagiri

31465

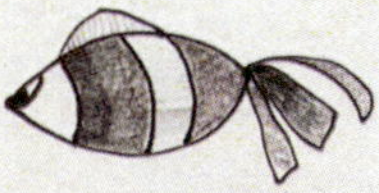

POST CARD

PLACE STAMP HERE

I wish you were
here tooo! :)

here NO Varkala →

Varkala thaaat
← side

Jeste joging
Varkala
this saaide only

Cheta's coconuts 18-11-90

Anandan 18-11-90

Surfers Camp 18-11-90

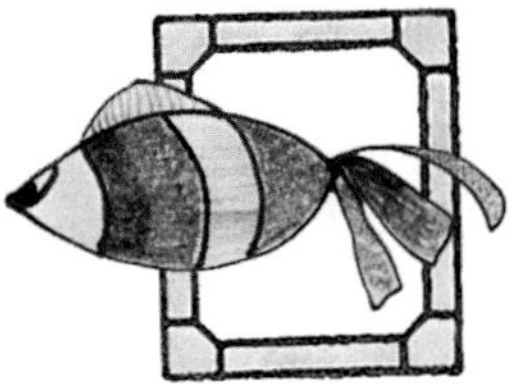

A TRUNK FULL OF WATER

Varkala

'Varkala, please?' asked Candida.

The coconut seller on the wayside frowned, securing his lungi more firmly around his waist and wiping the sweat off his brow. It was the end of November, almost winter, so Kerala was hot. In the summer, it was boiling.

'Varkala, you are asking, aanh?' the coconut seller demanded.

Candida nodded. She shifted her weight from her left leg to her right to keep the Royal Enfield beneath her from listing too much to one side.

'No-no-no-no-no meydum, sooori. Wryoong nember.'

It took a few moments for Candida to register that the man had spoken English, so thick had the Malayali accent been on his tongue. It took her another moment to understand that he had said: *Sorry madam, wrong number.*

Did he mean that she had come to the wrong place, then?

'Here no Varkala. Varkala *thaat* saaide,' he said, pointing north.

That side? Which side? She had travelled from Rajasthan into Gujarat, Maharashtra, Goa, then Karnataka, drinking in sights of temples and forests, and the cloud-kissed hills of the western ghats. She revelled in the solitude of wind, sand and ocean as she rode. The same Arabian Sea looked so different in each place, displaying moods and colours and ever-changing depths near the coast as Candida travelled further and further South. At last she reached Kollam and finally made it into the Thiruvananthapuram district of Kerala. In fact, the city of Trivandrum couldn't be above forty kilometres ahead on this road. Then why did the coconut seller point her in a different direction?

Candida started to feel desperate. Had she ridden all this way for nothing? She had so wanted to visit the little town of Varkala, which she had heard was like a small jewel perched on the luscious coastline of the southern-most state of India. A friend who was familiar with Kerala had told her to address all unknown men as 'chata', meaning elder brother in Malayalam. She tried again.

'Chata, please, where is Varkala?'

The coconut seller peered into her face. Satisfying himself that he had sufficiently flummoxed this pretty young lady, he threw his head back and laughed in hearty enjoyment of his little trick. When he was done, he winked and said, 'Jeste joging, aanh? Varkala this saaide only.'

Okay, so he was just joking and Varkala is this side only, thought Candida drily. *Kudos on a great sense of humour, chata! You are the elder brother I never had*, her brain grumbled sarcastically. Out loud she said nothing. By her calculations, Varkala shouldn't be far. As if reading her thoughts, the coconut seller grinned and held up ten fingers, then motioned to her bike. Oh good, she was nearly there! Just a ten-minute ride away.

'Thank you, chata,' she said and made to start the bike, when the man held out a tender coconut with a straw standing up invitingly from the cool waters contained inside it. Candida read genuine kindness in the man's eyes, and she accepted it with a smile. The drink was most refreshing. When she tried to pay him for it, he shook his head good-naturedly and waved her on her way.

And that was Candida Louis' introduction to that friendly cliff-side city of Varkala. It was love at first sight!

As she rode into Varkala twenty minutes later, a breath-taking view met her eyes. What lay before her was a sea with no beach. A city with no boundaries. There was Varkala, and there was the sea, and nothing else between them. Cafés and rest houses dotted the cliff's edge, looking as if they would, at any moment, dive into the Arabian Sea. Then, before Candida's stunned eyes, the sun decided to call it a day and plunged over the horizon, taking all the light from the world with it. Candida wandered for a while, wondering what to do next. Somewhere along the journey between Rajasthan and Kerala, and the many places she had visited along the way, her pockets were getting close to empty. She couldn't afford to spend too much money on accommodation. She'd need to find a cheap place to stay.

Then she met Siraj, owner of The Haven, the place she would come to call home for the next seven days. When she told him of her plans and what she had been doing—travelling across India on a motorcycle—he was fascinated.

'You can stay at our inn, madam,' he said.

'Er ... thank you. But first, could I just know how much it will cost ...' she broke off in embarrassment.

'It will cost you stories, madam,' replied Siraj with a sudden twinkle in his eye.

'I beg your pardon?' said Candida, wondering whether this rest house owner, like the coconut seller, was 'jeste joging' too.

Now Siraj smiled, and his smile reached all the way to his eyes. 'My wife and I would love to hear about your travels. There must be many stories about all the beautiful places you visited, no? In exchange, we will give you room. You stay, you eat with us, you tell us your adventures. Okay, madam?'

Candida grinned and nodded. 'It's a deal,' she said. Siraj took her inside and introduced her to his wife, Mira, then showed her to her room. It had blue walls, a cot, a side table and nothing else. But there was a floral motif painted on the wall behind the bed that grabbed Candida's heart. She knew at once that she would be happy staying here. She remembered what the shepherd at Pangmo had said to her. Allah baksh. This, too, like the fire that he had built her, and the soup his wife had cooked, was a gift from God ...

She looked around quickly and said, 'Thank you, Siraj!' He stopped at the door and turned.

'Alone you have travelled for so many days. You are a brave lady, madam,' he said quietly. 'God bless you.' He left the room, shutting the door softly behind him.

The next day, Mira told Candida about an elephant farm.

'What's that?' asked Candida, her curiosity thoroughly piqued. But even before Mira could tell her about Ananthavalam—a set-up by the river that was home to five elephants—Candida knew that Puthenkulam, where the farm was located, was going to be her destination that day. The idea of hanging out with elephants was just irresistible!

Breakfast was a leisurely affair. She dined with Siraj and Mira, and told them about Gurais. They listened, wide-eyed, while Siraj kept her plate supplied with delicious jaffles. She never noticed how much she ate or how much she spoke until she told them of how the officers had tried to recruit her to the army. This produced a guffaw from somewhere behind her left shoulder. Turning in surprise, Candida realized that she had an audience. An English couple, Jim and Sarah, along with three other tourists, had wandered up to join their little group, and had been listening to her adventures with as much attention as Siraj and Mira.

Jim smiled and held out his hand. He made the introductions, and Candida found herself liking him and Sarah at once. Jim had a pleasant face and a guitar slung over the back of his chair. Candida was to discover that he and his guitar were never far apart.

Suddenly recalling the time, Candida wrapped up her story, bid goodbye to her new friends and rose to go. That is when the weight of all those jaffles sitting in her tummy made their presence felt.

'Uff! Siraj! Keep feeding me like this and I'll never be able to leave from here!' groaned Candida clutching her middle and dropping back into the chair. Siraj grinned unrepentantly while Mira helped Candida to her feet. As she walked to the Royal Enfield parked under a tree, a voice called out from behind her, 'Hey, wait up!' Turning, she saw three individuals approaching – Jim, Sarah and Jim's Guitar.

'Siraj tells us you're heading to the elephant farm. We were going to go there ourselves. Mind if we join you?' asked Sarah.

'Not at all,' said Candida, brightly. 'I'll be glad of the company!'

The road to Puthenkulam passed through a most exquisite sight – the sea on one side, and a lake on the other. Candida pointed it out to her friends at the very same instant that they pointed it out to her! Lifting the wind guard on her helmet, she mouthed the words, 'We'll stop here on the way back?'

'Yes!' called Sarah, while Jim expressed his approval with a thumbs-up.

At Puthenkulam, an elephant called Anandan was about to begin his daily bath. True to his name, he seemed happy to be wallowing in the waters, while his mahout went about the business of scrubbing him clean. Candida stood by watching, but five minutes was all she could resist. She stepped forward eagerly, and the mahout looked up and saw her.

'Chata, please, may I help give him a bath?'

The mahout nodded and handed her a small bucket, before returning to what he was doing. Candida bent down and scooped water in the bucket. She yearned to touch the elephant, but was a little afraid. He was, after all, a fully-grown pachyderm that could, if he decided to, knock her over (or worse!) with a flick of his mighty trunk! But Anandan had other plans. When Candida splashed the water on his flank and bent to collect another bucketful, she was greeted by a spray of water to the side of her head, with a force that nearly toppled her over! She looked around quickly, wondering where that had come from. Anandan's trunk was pointed straight at her! It was him then, the rascal! Candida hurled the water in her bucket at him. Back came a spray, getting her in the face this time. Gasping and rubbing the water out of her eyes, she saw that the elephant was smiling cheekily at her. She burst out laughing, wrapping her arms around Anandan's trunk. The elephant stood there, looking absurdly pleased with himself!

This was an experience Candida would never forget. She liked Siraj and his wife, and Jim and Sarah immensely. But beyond a doubt, the best friend she had made on this trip was Anandan! She would keep in touch with the others on WhatsApp and Facebook. But this elephant, with whom she would share no words, whom she would probably never see again, would remain imprinted in her heart forever. Just like Tim.

On the ride back to Varkala, Jim, Sarah, Jim's Guitar and Candida visited the Kappil Lake. It was blue, which was unusual for lakes in this part of the country. The water bodies in South India tended to be brown or grey. There were some fishermen working by the waters, and the friends strolled up to them to see what they were about.

'Do you fish?' asked Jim of Candida.

'Never tried it,' she replied.

'Well, come on, then,' he urged. Through gestures, he conveyed to the fishermen that the ladies accompanying him would like to fish. His warm smile was irresistible, and the fishermen laughed and began to explain in rapid Malayalam how it was done. Candida and Sarah settled down to the task, sitting beside the lake holding their nets patiently. Meanwhile, Jim sat on a rock a little distance away and began to strum softly to himself. He was a quiet fellow who preferred to speak through the strings of his guitar rather than through words. But Sarah was more communicative.

As they sat waiting for the fish to stray into their nets, Sarah told Candida about their life in England. They had a married daughter in London, and an apartment that they had rented out to Airbnb. With the money they earned from it, they travelled the world.

'He's a music producer, you know?' Sarah told Candida, her eyes resting proudly on her husband, 'and quite a musician himself.' Candida smiled. These people were like her, wanderers in spirit, with the beat of adventure in their hearts.

After a while, Sarah too fell silent, and a gentle peace descended upon the place. A half-hour or so later, Candida suddenly felt a tug on her net and looked down quickly. There was a fish, struggling with all its might! She was about to alert the others, when her excitement suddenly turned to sadness. *Look at him struggle,* she thought. *How powerfully he thrashes that tiny body when there is his freedom to be gained. How precious life is even to a little creature.* Bending down, she lifted the writhing body from the confines of the net and gently placed it back into the safety of the water.

After all, this could have been Tim ...

They returned to the inn by sunset, empty-handed.

'I never have any luck with these things,' shrugged Sarah good-naturedly, 'but I was certain you would catch one at least.'

Candida smiled. 'I'm not lucky with these things either,' she replied, and said no more. After a much-needed bath, Candida emerged from her room to join Siraj and Mira. More stories followed—this time about Bali, where she headed bikers' expeditions from time to time—and then, tired out from the long day, Candida went to bed.

The rest of Candida's stay in Varkala passed in realizing a long-standing dream – SURFING!

She had imagined that the sport involved a surfboard, a surfer and a wave. She was wrong. On her second morning at Varkala, down by the coastline where a Surfers' Camp was conducting beginners' classes on the narrow strip of sand, Candida discovered that surfing involved days of training, and no contact with the water whatsoever at the outset. This was a hardship in itself for one who had jumped into the freezing waters of Chandra Tal within the first ten seconds of laying eyes on it!

But soon, Candida realized the necessity of all this preparation. Being out at sea all alone among the waves was no joke. On day two, three swimmers had taken on the ocean, and would have drowned but for the quick action of the lifeguards who went in after them and brought them back to safety. Much chastised by the scare this episode gave all of them, Candida kept her head down and applied herself most earnestly to the lessons being taught at the camp. Gradually, she learnt to keep her balance on a surfboard, first on land and then in shallow waters. She learnt to lie flat upon the surfboard and paddle out to sea until she found a good wave. By the fifth day, she could hop onto her surfboard when the wave came. By the sixth, she managed to crouch low on it with bended knees to keep from losing her balance.

On the seventh day, she rode her first wave.

And that was what was called SURFING!

By the end of her stay in Varkala, Candida had shared many stories, made friends she would keep for life, and even 'told' a funny song about a road trip on a bike that Jim recorded to background music, and produced for her into a music video when he returned to England! It was now time to stuff her belongings back into her haversack and be on her way. She would miss strolling along the cliff's edge, watching the spectacular sunsets. She would miss the salty smell of the sea in her hair, Siraj's jaffles, and the cafés Jim and Sarah and Jim's Guitar accompanied her to in the evenings. As she left the empty blue room, she reached out and touched the floral motif behind her bed one last time.

Goodbyes are never easy. But in these past months, Candida had learnt to keep her eyes on the road ahead. For, she had come to understand that looking back can cause a girl to fall off her bike and break her heart ...

STATE HIGHWAY 49

STATE HIGHWAY 49

Pondicherry

Candida had never seen the inside of a motorbike factory before. So, an invitation to visit one proved irresistible! Enfield had offered her a guided tour of their manufacturing unit in Poonamallee (on the outskirts of Chennai), and Candida had jumped at the opportunity. So here she was, one late November day, cutting her visit to Hampi short to head South to Chennai. She had covered close to 18,000 kilometres of travel across India since setting out from Hubballi in August, and once again another long and seemingly endless journey lay ahead of her – but then, as you know, Candida Louis was no stranger to them.

From Varkala, Candida had visited Kanyakumari, Dhanushkodi, Rameshwaram, Madurai and Kodaikanal. The abandoned town of Dhanushkodi was situated in Pamban Island, and formed a stretch of sandy embankment between India and Sri Lanka. Candida rode into the town and immediately got that sense of other-worldliness that Kuldhara in Rajasthan had given off. Disembarking from her bike, she walked along the stretch of sand, heading further south and east with every step. To her left was the Arabian Sea, and to her right, the Indian Ocean. Straight ahead, the sea stretched out blue and endless. Candida walked on until she reached the tip, the very tip of sand. Beyond this, there was nowhere to go. No left, no right, no longer a separation between two oceans, for there was no land left to separate them. From here, a little further into the blue waters, lay the island kingdom of the legendary king Ravana. Here, it is believed, Hanuman and Sugriva, with the help of their army of moneys, built a bridge for Rama and Lakshmana to cross the waters and rescue Sita from captivity.

Dhanushkodi was a place where two oceans met, the confluence of history, legend and mythology.

From Kodaikanal, Candida returned to Bangalore. After a brief stopover of just a day, she had then ridden out to Hampi in east-central Karnataka, where she was to meet up with friends, and visit that ancient capital of the prosperous 14th century Vijayanagara dynasty. She had heard much about the splendid temples and stone carvings of Hampi that perfectly synthesized the styles of the Hoysala, Chola, Pandya and Chalukya builders, and continued to impact the artistic consciousness of the South Indian people to this day. With so much to see and do, Candida's plan had been to remain at Hampi for a week at least.

The plan had been scuppered.

Four days into her stay, the invitation from the Enfield factory had arrived, and Candida had grabbed her haversack, bid a hasty goodbye to her friends and hit the road. Shrines and monuments could wait. She was off to visit the magical place where motorbikes were made! Since she would be going as far as Chennai, Candida decided that after the factory visit, she would travel further on to Pondicherry, a place she had long dreamed of exploring.

She arrived into Poonamallee late in the afternoon on the last day of November. Making her way directly to the Royal Enfield factory (where her arrival was awaited), she immediately lost herself in the world of engines and transmissions and suspensions! When she resurfaced, the sun had set and the manager was standing by impatiently, waiting to lock up.

'Oh! It's late. Maybe I should leave?' enquired Candida politely.

'Goodnight,' came the curt reply.

Candida knew a dismissal when she heard one. She shrugged good-naturedly and left. It wasn't until the iron gates had shut firmly behind her that she remembered that she had no place to go to. She stood around wondering what to do next, when the elderly night watchman asked her where she would stay. He spoke in Tamil, but Candida got his meaning and shook her head to indicate that she had no idea.

'Neenga showroom leiye irukalam, madam. Yarum varamaataanga.'

'Pardon?'

'Showroom there. You stay in showroom.'

He pointed to a place up the street where there was, indeed, a Royal Enfield showroom. Seeing her doubtful frown, the old man smiled.

'*Fullly* safety. You inside, I locking outside, yaarume varamataaru. No one botheration for you.'

That sounded like as good an option as any. Following a hurried meal of masala dosas at a small restaurant across the street, she returned to the night watchman, who walked her to the showroom, unlocked it and let her in. After she heard the key turn in the lock outside, she freshened up in the restroom meant for the showroom clients, stretched out on one of the sofas and fell asleep. She didn't stir until she heard the day watchman raise the shutters outside at 10 the next morning.

Coming abruptly awake at the sound, Candida pulled on her gear, grabbed her haversack and rushed to the door. The instant it swung open, she stepped outside into the rain. The day watchman jumped at the sight of a young lady in full biking gear emerging from a room he had believed to be empty. He stared after her, open-mouthed, but Candida knew better than to turn around.

'Keep walking,' she said to herself through clenched teeth. The delectable smell of sambar and chutney wafted her way from the restaurant. Her stomach responded with a growl.

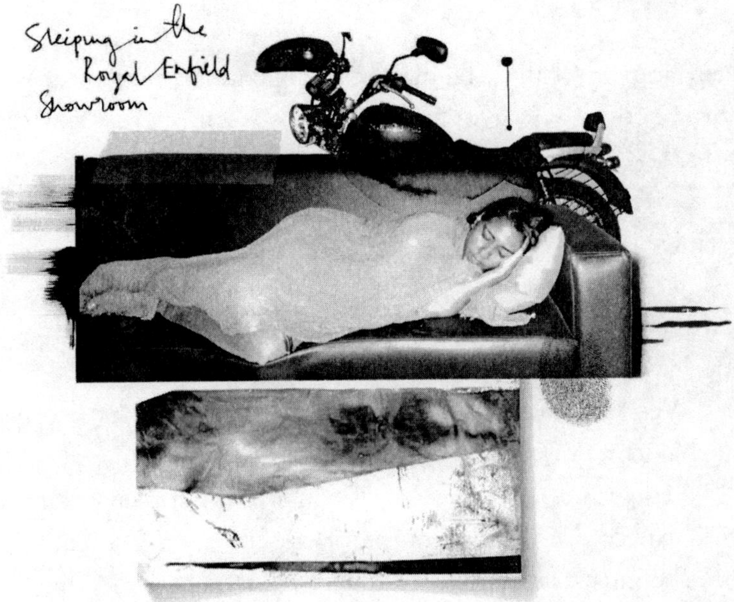

'Not now!' Candida reprimanded it sternly. She mounted her bike and, before the watchman could gather his wits, sped away!

The East Coast Road, also known as State Highway 49, links Chennai to the Union Territory of Pondicherry. Candida was well and truly on her way! A light rain continued to drop from the overcast skies. However, Candida, having ridden through Kerala downpours, dunked herself into the Chandra Tal, and been on the receiving end of an impromptu bath from an elephant, thought nothing of it. She rode on, and only stopped for a light breakfast of idlis and coffee at a wayside restaurant. 'Restaurant' was an exaggeration, really. The place was little more than a lean-to. But the coffee was strong and the idlis steaming hot, so they did nicely.

After a while, she noticed the shop owner eyeing her curiously.

'Pondicherry poga poreengala, madam?' he asked. She gathered that he was referring to her destination, so she nodded.

'Vendam, madam, pogatheengo. Mazhai, mazhai, neriya mazhai vara poguthu!'

His accompanying gestures conveyed that heavy rains were expected. He shook his hands vigorously to indicate that she must travel no further. He was so vehement, that Candida began to feel doubtful. What should she do? She had waited so long to visit Pondicherry—years in fact—and her sabbatical from her finance job in Bangalore was almost at an end. Still, the idli-seller's warning seemed hard to ignore ...

She turned the Royal Enfield back towards Chennai.

Then, seven kilometres along SH 49, Candida Louis was suddenly gripped by a strange inner compulsion. She stopped, checked the highway for oncoming traffic, turned around again, and rode all the way to Pondicherry without stopping.

It was the evening of 30th November, 2015, when Candida entered the Union Territory of Pondicherry on the south-eastern coast of India. She had been on the road for close to four months and had never yet had a problem finding a place to sleep in. That day, for the first time, things went differently. She parked the bike and made her way to the ocean. Her pocket and her spirit of adventure, both, answered to any one of the numerous shacks that lined the beach – the most popular accommodation among tourists on a tight budget. Beginning at the head of the beach, she walked down the line, approaching the more appealing shacks to seek shelter. Each one of them informed her that they were not taking any guests at present. She was a little puzzled. Now, she approached the lesser known ones. There, too, she received the same answer. Finally, in desperation, she asked the man in charge of one place, 'Are you fully booked? I can't seem to find a place to stay.'

'Not fully full, madam. Fully empty. We are on cyclone alert and we are not allowed to take in guests because we are too close to the sea.'

'But—'

'No but, madam. That is the situation,' he cut her off impatiently.

'Please! Can't you help me? Just for one night?'

'Nobody can help you. All have to vacate within the next few minutes.'

'Maybe the local fisherfolk will let me stay with them then ...?' she trailed off when she saw him looking at her oddly.

'You don't understand, madam?' he said quietly, at last. 'There are no fisherfolk here. They were evacuated to safe areas yesterday.'

Candida had never witnessed a cyclone, having only lived in landlocked cities all her life, and therefore couldn't fully comprehend what he was talking about. It was the kind of thing one read about in newspapers over a cup of coffee in the morning.

It was now past 10 p.m. For the first time in months, Candida felt the stirrings of real fear ...

She made her way along the beach, back towards town. Rain was beating down briskly now, and the wind was strong, whipping her hair around her head and into her eyes. Finally, she pulled on her helmet. At the head of the beach, she turned around in the buffeting gale to look at the long line of shacks she had left behind. Not a light shone from any of them, save the one she had just left. As she watched, the light in that one went off too. Now, all was darkness.

Hurrying along, Candida ducked under the awning of a closed shop and pulled out her phone. She typed the words: 'Pondicherry on cyclone alert. No accommodation. Low on cash. HELP!' She posted it on the family WhatsApp group and then sat down on the shop step. Her mind was numb, her body bone weary. She dropped her head into her hands and stayed that way until a series of beeps alerted her to messages pouring in. When she checked, she found crying emojis, worried enquiries, recriminations from a bossy cousin over the stupidity of travelling to a place without checking the weather reports first!

Another beep. Candida glanced absently at the screen and found a message from Aunt Carissa. 'The manager of Hotel Park International is expecting your call. Mention Uncle Patrick's name.'

This message was followed by a mobile number. Candida immediately dialled it.

'Miss Louis?' said the manager without preamble.

'Er ... yes, Candida here. I'm—'

'Madam, please come over, your room is ready.'

She started to thank him, but realized that he had rung off.

Google Maps led her straight to Kamaraj Salai, the road on which the hotel was situated. She stopped and stared up at the nicely lit white-and-glass façade of the 3-star hotel. She couldn't stay here! She couldn't possibly afford it!

But the rain had intensified considerably and soaked her to the skin. Even parked as she was, she could feel the

Royal Enfield listing to one side under the relentless wind. She didn't have a choice.

In the lobby, the manager was bustling around trying to make the necessary arrangements for the hotel and its guests to weather the oncoming storm. Nevertheless, he kept an eye out for Candida, and claimed her the moment she approached the front desk. His welcome was hurried but kind. She badly wanted to ask how much a room here would cost, but he gave her no time. He ushered her and the bellboy into the lift, put the key into the latter's hand, and returned to business even before the lift doors could close.

The room was, well ... splendid! There was no other word for it, seeing it, as she was, through eyes that had grown accustomed to shacks, wayside inns, dormitories and hostels in these past months on the road. The bellboy, Senthil was smiling expectantly at her, and she suddenly remembered that in places like these, a tip was protocol. She dived into her haversack, came up with a twenty and offered it to him. His expression changed to one of horror.

'No-no-no-no, madam, vendam, madam! Neenga enna sapadreenga? Food, food?'

She smiled and shook her head. Her extravagance in choosing to remain in this hotel would cost her dearly, she knew, not that she had much of a choice. But she wasn't going to compound the error by ordering from the hotel's fancy menu.

'No, thank you, I already ate,' she lied smilingly, even while her stomach rumbled traitorously with hunger. Senthil looked at her quietly for a moment, then nodded and left.

Candida went into the bathroom and revelled in a hot shower. 'First thing tomorrow, I will check out of here and find some food,' she promised herself. 'The weather should clear up by then.'

She was just preparing for bed when there was a discreet knock on the door. Hurrying out of bed, she looked through the peep hole. There was nobody there. She frowned. Had she imagined it? She opened the door cautiously. The corridor was empty. Then, something lying by the side of the door caught her eye. A tray full of food! Surprised, she picked it up and carried it inside to the coffee table beside the bed. Lifting off the metal lids and warmers revealed dishes of paneer, roti, daal and salad. With the prospect of food before her, Candida could finally admit how famished she truly was! She smiled to herself, once again remembering the shepherd at Pangmo and his words.

'Thank you,' she whispered to the kindness that had sent her this meal. She began to eat.

The room was dark when Candida opened her eyes. Was it still night? She glanced at her phone. 9.23 a.m. The heavy curtains drawn across the bay windows had entirely obliterated the morning light! Getting dressed in a hurry, Candida made her way down to the reception with her haversack. She needed to begin looking for an affordable place as soon as possible.

The doors of the elevator parted, and Candida's eyes immediately fell on the front entrance across the lobby. The sight that met her eyes made her jaw drop open. Mist! Dense, grey mist had shrouded the world. The hotel staff was huddled at the entrance, pointing to something outside in apparent distress. Candida hurried over to get a better look ... and stopped still in horror. What she had thought to be mist was, in fact, an impenetrable blanket of rain, beating down in torrents. The Bay of Bengal in the distance had risen, writhing and thrashing, to swallow up the beach. It was as if the very sky had collapsed into the sea, with no material separation between the two. Tall coconut trees bent dangerously low, strained to hold on to the ground beneath them. But the cause of all the alarm was the person on the other side of the hotel doors, clinging desperately to a lamp post to keep from being blown away! Candida found herself praying frantically, fervently, as she watched, while someone tethered himself firmly to a pillar at the entrance with thick ropes, and braved the wind to go out and rescue the man! When he got his arms firmly around the man's body, the hotel staff hauled both of them inside to safety. A shout of joy went around the room, and Candida found tears of terror and relief running down her cheeks as she clapped and cheered with the rest.

Mattresses, a sari, a child's vest, a doll, kitchen utensils and household articles from the evacuated fishing villages nearby were lifted up and tossed into the sky by the strong winds. They remained there for a second or two before they were swept from sight forever.

'This could have been me ...' thought Candida numbly. For the first time, it sank into her dazed mind what a cyclone could do, what she had narrowly escaped the previous night. She was grateful that, while she had been worrying about money and doubting her circumstances, Fate had conspired to save her life. Allah baksh ... Her very existence, now, was a gift from God. She felt humbled.

By evening, the rain paused to catch its breath. It was the proverbial lull before the next storm, and when the hotel staff told her so, she did not make the mistake of disbelieving them.

'It will come back, madam. Again it will start,' they assured her.

Still, she couldn't resist seizing the opportunity to grab the Royal Enfield and take a quick tour of the town. She knew she had an hour at best, and promised herself that the minute the drizzle started to turn to rain, she would head right back to the hotel. She rode through Auroville, taking in the beautiful buildings, the quaint streets, riding past the Aroma Gardens and stopping for a minute to stare in fascination at the Matrimandir with its splendid golden discs that shone dully in the grey light. *Imagine how it would be in bright sunshine*, thought Candida, before riding on. Suddenly, she remembered Spike telling her about the brownies at the Auroville Bakery that he had eaten the year before when he had visited with friends. Her mouth watered at the thought, and even though the light drizzle was slowly picking up in pace, she pulled up outside the bakery and went inside.

The establishment was pleasant, modern, and surprisingly crowded. Tourists and locals—Indians and foreigners alike—were evidently taking advantage of the respite from the rain, just as she was. Candida ducked her head to hide a smile. It felt good to know that there were others in the world as foolish as she, who would do anything for the taste of a good brownie! She joined the queue, frequently raising herself on tiptoe to check how many brownies were left. Spike had told her that they sold out within the first hour, like the proverbial hot cakes!

When she was two people away from reaching the head of the queue, the last of the brownies vanished. There was a general groan of disappointment, and people slowly began to disperse. Suddenly someone called, 'Hey!'

Everyone turned. A foreigner holding a box addressed the room in an American accent. 'People here braved some pretty rough weather to get a taste of these brownies. I say that we don't let them leave without it!'

Everyone looked at him uncomprehendingly. He grinned.

'I say that those of us who bought more than one brownie put our extra ones down on this table and let those who didn't get any help themselves. I'm going to begin by putting this box of mine down. There are ten brownies in here ...' He picked one out. 'Now nine!' As he spoke, the American took a bite of his share with a cajoling smile.

In a flash, the mood in the room changed to one of warmth and gaiety. People hurried forward with their contributions. Within moments, the table was piled high with brownies, enough to go around. Thrilled, Candida stepped forward and helped herself. Taking her baseball cap out of her haversack, she overturned it on the table and put twenty-five rupees into it—the cost of one piece of brownie—to encourage everyone to pay for what they took. Then, dropping a quick, impulsive kiss on the surprised American's cheek, she hurried out to her bike and rode back to Park International, just as the rain began to pound the earth again.

Upstairs, in the warmth of her room, Candida stretched out on her big luxurious bed. She took her first bite of the brownie and sighed. Spike was right. It was the 'deliciousest' brownie in the world! Her phone beeped. She glanced at the message. It was from her boss at work.

'Your sabbatical gets over in 5 days,' the message read. 'If you don't report to work by then, HR asks that you hand in your resignation.'

The finality of the words was unmistakable. Stuck as she was in this sort of weather, there wasn't much that she could do at the moment. But she knew that she would have to leave the minute the weather cleared. Besides her job, she could not afford to stay longer than necessary in as expensive a place as this.

Four days later, the cyclone having spent itself, finally moved on leaving behind only an incessant drizzle in its wake. Rains were predicted to lighten over the next few days. Candida went downstairs armed with her credit card. She'd try to earn the money back once she returned to Bangalore. She approached the manager and handed him her card.

'I must leave, sir. But I am more grateful than I can say for your kindness in past few days. I don't know what would have happened if you hadn't helped me.'

'Probably blown away to Sri Lanka?' suggested the manager with a twinkle in his eye.

'Probably!' laughed Candida. He still hadn't taken her credit card. She offered it to him again, and he looked down at it for a long moment. 'Your uncle helped to open the first of these hotels, madam,' he said quietly. 'Since then, our owner has gone on to build twelve others. How can we charge Mr Joseph's niece for staying with us? She is our guest, and we are honoured to have her with us.'

Candida said nothing. There was a tightness in her throat that wouldn't allow her to speak. Once again she held out the card.

'Please ...' she reasoned hoarsely, 'that is between you and my uncle. I have nothing to do with ... *Please!*'

Suddenly, the manager laughed. 'Do you want me to lose my job, madam?'

Candida couldn't laugh with him. She couldn't even summon up a smile. She shook her head and said only two words: 'Thank you.' But she said it in a tone that conveyed her gratitude to the fullest.

As Candida Louis rode away from Pondicherry, the clouds were still hanging low over the city, and the light was a silvery grey. Trees had fallen everywhere, walls had collapsed, electric poles had toppled onto vehicles and crushed them. Debris lay everywhere. Candida's heart clenched. Instinctively, she knew that she would never see Pondicherry again. Her work here was done. People visited places to see them at their best. She had seen Pondicherry at its worst. And she couldn't imagine loving it more than she did at that moment.

CANDID CHAT

An Interview with Candida Louis

One day in 2019, while in Hubballi on a visit to her parents, Candida visited an orphanage on the request of the priest of her parish. An elderly gentleman and his daughter ran the place and took in children of all age groups. They had heard much about Candida from the priest, and thought it would be inspiring for the older children in the group, who were on the brink of choosing their career paths, to meet a person like her. Candida was happy to oblige. The questions below are based on the interaction she had with them, as they were recorded by the elderly gentleman.

Divyashree: *What was your childhood like? Were you close to your parents and siblings?*

Candida: I grew up an only child in a middle-class Anglo

Indian family in Hubballi. We lived in a matchbox-sized house in the beginning. But I remember my parents always working hard to give me a better life. I started working from the age of eighteen itself, because I always wanted to give back to my parents for all their efforts, and start looking after myself as early as possible. We were a very close-knit family. (Smiles) We still are.

As a single child, growing up was fun but sometimes lonely. My parents were busy with work, but I had my doggy, Fluffy, who was more like a sibling to me! It is probably because of this that I enjoy riding out to secluded places for peace and time alone, away from the noise and crowd of big-city life. I also always end up with a friendly dog-companion wherever I go, which is nice.

My parents have always been more like friends to me. I could tell them everything I did and they would guide me. Over the years, we've built that trust between us, which is very, very important, especially since I'm away from them, working and travelling, most of the time.

Manjunath: *What inspired you to go on this journey?*

Candida: As a kid, I always dreamt of riding around the world on a motorcycle. But it was very difficult for me to take that first big step – giving up my stable job at a company. Also, I didn't have the funds. Then, one day at work, I received a call from a friend, who said that they were filming a travel series around India and were looking for a biker. I knew this was my chance to take that risk, since all the expenses would be covered. I took a sabbatical from work to ride around India. But that trip lasted only for twenty days, and I had several more months of leave in hand. I decided to continue travelling by myself, because I would never again get such an opportunity.

Maanya: *Did your parents ever get frightened that you were travelling alone?*

Candida: I started travelling alone when I was quite young. I had family and friends in different parts of the country, so I would visit them during my summer vacations. And most of those flight and train journeys I would take on my own.

When I set out on this ride, my parents were very scared initially. So, I made sure I updated them daily, and informed them in advance when travelling to places without network. I also explained to them that if I could ride through Spiti Valley (which has some of the most treacherous roads in India) then other places would never be a problem!

However, it did take a while for them to get used to the idea. I had to prove to them that I could handle difficult situations and take care of myself on the road. Also, being devout Catholics, they really have faith in God and know that he will protect me. I'm grateful to them for believing in me. I wouldn't be able to do what I do without their support.

Shreya: *Did you ever feel scared or unsafe while travelling?*

Candida: Several times! (Chuckles) Once when I encountered a ghost!

Shreya: *What happened??*

Candida: I had ridden from Kolkata to Siliguri for fourteen hours through bad roads, rain and traffic. It was 2 a.m. when my fellow-bikers and I reached Siliguri, and we were totally exhausted. I was shown to my room, which was on the top floor of a hotel that had once been a school. The building was more than a hundred-and-thirty years old, the lift still had a lever system to go up and down, and the walls looked very beaten up. I took a shower and climbed into bed. But as soon as I laid my head on the pillow, I heard a loud knocking sound right behind my head. When I got up to see what it was, the knocking stopped. I closed my eyes again. This time the knocking was even louder. It was as if someone was banging on the headboard. It gave me quite a fright. I went out to check the balcony adjoining the room, but there was no one there. At 3 in the morning, even the street below was deserted. I went back to bed. But every time I lay my head on the pillow, the knocking would start. When I raised it, the knocking would stop. I realized that this was no ordinary sound. So, I said a prayer, gathered my courage, and then said out loud to whoever was doing it: 'I am only here to stay for one night and I mean no harm. All I want to do is rest. I will leave in the morning.'

When I lay down again, the noise completely stopped! I slept very peacefully ... or rather, I should say that I was *allowed* to sleep very peacefully after that! (Laughs) Looking back, it was a really scary experience.

Manjunath: *Any other memories of being scared while you were on the road?*

Candida: Sometimes during my travels, I wouldn't be able to find a place to stay the night. So I would have to continue riding through the night to reach a big city and find decent accommodation. Riding in complete darkness through tiny village roads gave me the chills, like the time I rode on the Delhi-Agra highway at 1 in the morning. That highway is notorious for its murders, actually. Anyway, soon I learnt to plan my routes better, where I'd leave early and reach my destination before sunset.

Another time I felt unsafe was when I arrived in Patna. A group of bikers were waiting at the hotel to welcome me. After we exchanged pleasantries, I wanted to go to my room. They were being overly friendly, and I didn't feel comfortable with them. But instead of leaving, the whole lot of them followed me upstairs. Then, before I knew it, there were about ten strange men crowding inside my room. It freaked me out. I waited for them to come out and only then did I enter the room and latch the door. Overall, I didn't get a good feeling from the place. I left Patna the very next morning!

Then, there was Madurai. When I reached Madurai, Navaratri celebrations were on in full swing, and tourists had flooded the city to visit the famous Madurai Meenakshi temple. Every single hotel was booked up. After roaming the streets for almost two hours, I finally managed to find myself a room. But then, I soon found out why it had been available – the door of this room didn't have a latch! I settled for it, since there was no other option and it was already 9 p.m.. I made sure to push my cot and everything else that was heavy and movable in the room up against the door. Throughout the night, people kept knocking. And with every knock I would come wide awake with fright. Of course, I never opened the door. Like Patna, Madurai was another place I left very quickly!

There were many more instances when I felt unsafe or scared. As I travelled, my instincts became sharper. I learnt how to read people better, to avoid deserted or lonely places, or places that didn't give me a good feeling; to conduct myself in a way that would not attract too much attention; to leave early and reach my destinations before sunset. Through it all, I knew that God was always watching over me, and I could feel his presence constantly.

Sumitra: *Any close calls?*

Candida: I had originally planned on riding from Kolkata to Siliguri following the route suggested by Google Maps. Early one morning, just as I was setting out, a friend called and informed me that there were two other bikers—Sohan

Roy sir from Pune and Raheem from Kolkata—making the same trip later that day. He suggested that I join them. I was already acquainted with the biking legend – Lt Col Sohan Roy (which biking enthusiast isn't?). I said to myself, 'When will I get the opportunity to ride with a pro like him again?' So I postponed my departure and left with them at 10 a.m. It was a fourteen-hour journey, by a different route than the one I had originally planned to take. I think somebody up there must have been watching out for me, because I discovered that Sohan sir had picked this route because the one Google Maps had suggested was crawling with Naxalites! God only knows what would have happened to me if I had been out there on those terrible roads alone, and that too after dark!

Shabaaz: *Any advice for people who are planning to travel alone like you are doing?*

Candida: To begin with, I would advise that you travel in groups, with family or friends. Every trip will increase your confidence and make you stronger.

For most of you, I'd say: Go on and do it! Don't be afraid of the unknown. Travel will energize your mind and change you in extraordinary ways. While you are travelling, make the right decisions and leave minimum carbon footprint. Be a responsible traveller.

Daniel: *What's the best food you've eaten, and where?*

Candida: Cheese naan in Surat was buttery and delicious! I went completely veg during my time there, and didn't even feel the need to eat non-veg. Aside of that, I must say that the memory of tundey kebab, butter chicken, chicken tikka ... well, actually, *all* the Avadhi food I ate in Lucknow, still makes my mouth water! In direct contrast, noodles cooked in Sprite when I had no water at a camp site was great fun too!

Apoorva: *If one were to take a trip and had a limited budget and time, which place would you recommend?*

Candida: If you plan your trips well and if you know how to spend wisely, then being on the road can actually be quite a lot cheaper than staying in a big city like Bangalore, where you tend to spend a lot more. I find most of the places in north India quite reasonable. And now, with the rise of Zostel and other such hostels designed especially for backpackers, travel is getting increasingly easy and cheap. My recommendations? Let's see ... Chikkamagalur in Karnataka, Rishikesh in Uttarakhand, Udaipur in Rajasthan, and Allepey in Kerala. Not all on the same journey, of course! (Laughs)

Shabaaz: *Can you tell us about some unusual or interesting people you met on your travels?*

Candida: (Smiling) You mean aside of the ghost in Kolkata? Hmm ... well, there was another ghost ... no, I'm not kidding, seriously ... another one I encountered in the dark, forested hills of Coorg, where I was visiting with friends. I was riding some distance behind the others, when a voice screamed in my ear: 'Take me!' I was so terrified, I stopped the bike right there and looked all around, but there was nobody.

Shreya: *What did you do, then?!*

Candida: (Laughing) What would you do if a ghost spoke to you from the darkness?

Shreya: *Run!*

Candida: Exactly! I ran ... or rather, *rode* ... for my life, to get away as quickly as possible! Anyway, that was about the ghosts I met. Among the living, I found a fisherman in Rameshwaram very interesting. While his wife was preparing lunch for us, we spoke about how he makes a living. He told me that aside of fishing, he was also a teacher, a snorkelling expert, and an organic farmer. It just shows that if you're passionate about something, and if you put your mind to it and really work hard, you can do wonders!

Divyashree: *What has your experience with social media been like? You use it a lot, don't you?*

Candida: At first, I started using social media to keep my parents and family updated about my whereabouts when I was travelling alone. For the large part, social media has been great because it has put me in contact with so many people who are interested in my travels and the work I do, and helped me to connect and collaborate with them. The encouragement and support that I have received from the biking community has been amazing! I know I am safe all over India and the world because of them.

But then, there have been a few bad experiences. To name one, quite recently (in July, 2018), I posted pictures of my 2015 visit to Chandra Tal in Spiti valley. When people saw the pics of me swimming in the lake, quite a few grew agitated and sent back photographs of signboards around the lake that banned swimming in it. There were a lot of hate messages about my harming mother nature. I immediately responded that those signboards were recent additions and hadn't been there back in 2015 when I had visited. That didn't seem to make a difference, people continued to send nasty and accusatory messages. I felt really bad, because I'm a responsible traveller. I think it's the carelessness that people have shown towards our natural resources that necessitate the rules to change so often.

In a nutshell, social media is a double-edged sword. There's so much good in it, so many advantages. But then, your experience with it can suddenly flip and go the other way. One has to be careful with what one expresses and shares publicly, for fear of being misunderstood. (Smiles) You live and learn!

ACKNOWLEDGEMENTS

This book was born of the foresight and dogged determination of Anamika, who has the ability to identify a goal and make a beeline for it. For introducing Candida to me, for suggesting the idea of a book on her travels, and for kick-starting Candid Tales (through kicking and starting, quite literally!), I owe her many hugs and a life-time supply of Agra Pethas!

Dr. Mohan Rao, Latha Nair, Haripriya Padmanabhan, Gopal Shankarnarayanan, Anamika and Prashant, in different ways, gently steered this book out of troubled waters and safely to the shore. This isn't the first time they have had to bail me out. I sheepishly admit that it may not be the last! I owe them all, and in particular Latha, my love and gratitude!

After I had unsuccessfully approached several editors with the concept of a travelogue for adults (and been turned down with alacrity!), Praveen suddenly planted in my brain the thought of writing these stories for children. It was a stroke of brilliance, and he came up with it because he cared. (Caring is the thing he does best, making it my good fortune that I share a home with him!) Tina picked up the idea and